THE EARL OF PEMBROKE

A League of Rogue's novel

LAUREN SMITH

*L*auren
SMITH
TIMELESS ROMANCE

ISBN: 978-1-947206-24-3 (e-book edition)

ISBN: 978-1-947206-25-0 (print edition)

For my grandmother Rhea and my grandfather Richard. They showed me what it means to love someone so much you carry their burdens as your own.

L ondon in the day was a bustling city with carriages speeding along the cobblestoned streets and women selling flowers in heavily perfumed baskets while the crowds perused the shops and paid calls on friends. But as darkness fell, shadows could play tricks on the eyes of those foolish enough to walk the streets after the sun dropped beneath the horizon.

And I am one of those fools.

Gillian Beaumont squinted at the nearest alley, swallowing hard and holding back a scream of fear every time she thought she saw something fluttering in the mews like a bat's wings. The coach she had taken to the Temple Bar district was already rattling away, leaving her alone. The leaves of the early fall scuttled along the ground, tangling in her skirts like brown spiders, making her jump. She gripped her gown below her knees and gave the fabric a shake, trying to loosen the dried leaves from her dark purple satin gown. Then she faced her surroundings. She stood on the street close to the Royal Courts of Justice and the entrance to Twinings tea shop.

Through the heavy gloom she could see the gilded sign that read *Twinings*, and she could just make out the two Chinese gentlemen sculpted into the stone above the tea shop's name. Their faces seemed fierce in the shadows, and Gillian looked away, turning her attention to the tall black form of the griffin statue that now looked more like a dragon because the shadows played tricks on her eyes.

In that moment she wished she was back in her warm bed. Asleep. Asleep and dreaming of one particular man and the stolen kisses they'd shared that kept pushing into her consciousness.

James Fordyce. The Earl of Pembroke was a dashing gentleman with a heart of gold and the warmest brown eyes she'd ever seen. She could still feel her hands threading through the strands of his dark hair as he kissed her in the corner of a bookshop and whispered poetry to her. He was everything she'd dreamed of but could never have. She was a servant and could be nothing more than that. A pang deep in her chest made her catch her breath, but she straightened her shoulders, shrugging off the pain, something she'd been trained to do for many years.

As dangerous as a dream of James was to her equilib-rium, it was a far sight safer than what she was currently engaged in—chasing after her wild, headstrong mistress, Audrey Sheridan.

Audrey was this very night attempting to expose a group of scoundrels who belonged to a hellfire club known as the Unholy Sinners of Hell. Such a dreadful name for a dreadful group of gentlemen. As a lady's maid, Gillian's duties ought to have been limited to tasks like dressing Audrey, preparing her for the day, and coming up with new ways to style her hair. She should *not* be sneaking about the Strand after dark in a domino half mask and a dark purple evening gown with an impossibly low bodice, searching for a group of dangerous men who were rumored to seduce virgins and make sacrifices to the devil.

"Heavens, Audrey, what have you gotten us into?" Gillian muttered to herself. She hastily examined the addresses of the buildings nearby, recalling the location from a letter Audrey had shown her earlier that morning which contained directions to the club.

The letter said the club was inside a tall white building two doors down from Twinings tea shop. The door knocker was an iron gargoyle's face sneering at all visitors. As she reached the rather unremarkable structure that supposedly housed a den of devil worshipers, Gillian studied the door. Her heart tripped a few beats as nerves threatened to freeze her in place.

There was no other option than to go inside. Audrey, her wayward mistress, was also her friend, and earlier that evening she had promised Gillian she would not go to this place. Yet when Gillian had awoken and found Audrey gone, she knew where her mistress must have gone.

She lied to me. No doubt out of some silly notion that she's protecting me, but she isn't.

Gillian would have charged into the fires of hell to protect her mistress. They were the same age, only nineteen, and in another life they might have been close friends, meeting for tea at Gunter's or going off to balls together.

In another life... If she had been born an heiress to her deceased father's estate instead of the daughter of an earl's mistress.

Her half brother, Adam, was now the Earl of Morrey, and her half sister, Caroline, didn't even know she existed. The previous Earl of Morrey had been careful in keeping his longtime mistress, Gillian's mother, well set up in a house in Mayfair and had even seen to Gillian's education, but even with such aid, her future had held limited options.

Gillian raised a gloved hand to the grotesque gargoyle and rapped the knocker twice loudly. Her breath held fast in her lungs, and she waited, her body shaking at the thought of the nature of the men inside. When the door finally opened, a grim-faced butler looked her up and down, before his lips curled back in a cruel smile.

"A little late, but 'tis no matter. They've plenty of energy tonight to see to *every* lady." He waved for her to enter. Gillian hesitated before taking a tentative step forward. Her skin crawled as the butler came too close when he closed the door, sealing her inside. She tried not to think about what his greeting suggested.

"This way." The butler led her down the corridor to a chamber and opened a door for her to enter. The drawing room, if indeed it could be called that, was outlandishly decorated with dark brocade furniture and red satin walls. These dubious men were certainly trying to create a sinful and seductive atmosphere, but rather than tasteful, it seemed crass. Yet they were clearly prepared for guests. A fire was lit, and a tea tray was on the table.

"Freshly brewed," the butler assured her. "Help yourself. When they are ready, you will be summoned."

Gillian murmured her thanks and settled herself on the couch. She reached up again to make sure the domino mask hadn't slipped. It was still fixed securely over her features.

Where was Audrey?

She had left half an hour before Gillian woke, according to the other servants in the Sheridan household. Had she sought out the protective escort of Charles Humphrey as she'd said she planned to? Gillian dearly hoped so. Otherwise, Audrey was putting herself at great risk. The Earl of Lonsdale was an eminently trustworthy gentleman, but he had a wicked reputation that would allow him entry to this club.

Earlier that day Gillian and Audrey had been warned by a man of their acquaintance not to seek out this hellfire club tonight. One of its members, Gerald Langley, had vowed vengeance upon Audrey—or rather, upon Lady Society, Audrey's anonymous identity as the writer of a social column. She had destroyed his reputation. Her remarks in the Lady Society column had been accurate and honest, but the outright cut direct from all of the *ton* against Langley had made him desperate for revenge.

Fortunately, he did not know Audrey was Lady Society; that was at least one small blessing. But Audrey and Gillian had been warned that Langley would lure Lady Society to his devil's lair with the threat of debauching virgins against their will, among other things, and Audrey was not the sort of woman to turn back on a challenge. But they'd had a plan, one they'd made together earlier that morning. They were to reach out to a few female members of that silly hellfire club and switch places with them for a proper payment. Yet after the adventures of the day and the dangers Gillian had faced when a man had attacked her, a man she suspected was in league with Gerald Langley, Audrey had promised to abandon the plan of going to the club tonight. Yet when Gillian had woken from her rest, she'd found her mistress gone. Had Audrey contacted one of those women? Surely she had.

Gillian stood and paced about the room, worry growing in the pit of her stomach. She didn't like that she was alone and liked even less that she didn't know where Audrey was. They were supposed to be here together, facing the dangers of this club side by side. She bit her lip nervously and after a moment decided to have a quick cup of tea. She hastily prepared a cup and drank it, hoping to calm her nerves. Then she set it down, hating the bitterness and wishing there had been sugar, but there hadn't even been a pitcher of milk. Only true devils would serve tea without access to milk and sugar.

Gillian was unable to ignore the stifling heat from the fire. The house around her was silent except for the occasional bark of distant male laughter from another room. Each time she heard that sound she tensed.

Part of the wall suddenly detached and revealed itself to be a door. A figure in black breeches, a white shirt, and a black waistcoat emerged. He wore a domino mask that had the delicate outline of a devil's features painted in red over the black.

"Good evening, my dear," the man purred as he held out a hand to her. His long fingers were white and strangely menacing.

Gillian gulped. "My friend and I were supposed to be here together. She will be wearing a red dress. Has she arrived yet?"

"Ah..." The man's lips twitched. "The lady in the red dress. She is here, waiting for you." The mask did little to hide the cruelty in his eyes, and she shivered.

"Waiting?" Gillian wished she had even a tiny inkling of what was about to happen, but she didn't. She was running headlong into this dark and dangerous world of devils.

The man curled the fingers of his still-open hand, beckoning her. "Yes, we are about to begin the feast."

Gillian came toward him, and he reached down and took one of her gloved hands. She allowed him to lead her into darkness.

JAMES FORDYCE, THE EARL OF PEMBROKE, STARED AT the card tables in the private gathering place of what London knew existed only in rumors. The Wicked Earls' Club. Members could be identified by a small silver pin they wore in their cravats. Once it had been a guild of prominent and powerful men who met in secret to make deals and curry favor, but their purpose had dissolved into a more corrupt world. It was not a place of malevolence or evil, but as James considered the men around him, their eyes locked on the flipping cards, the bottles abundant on the tables and the occasional woman draped over men's arms, breasts spilling over to please the eyes of every man in the room, there was a darkness of a kind here. The darkness that came from broken lost souls.

Souls like mine.

A dark figure loomed in the back of the room, and James recognized him, the leader of their club, the Earl of Coventry. Coventry gave James a small nod in silent greeting. James returned the nod and surveyed the room again. The ranks of the club had thinned in recent years, and he smiled at the thought of so many of his friends settling down with wives. Marriage to good women had a way of keeping men away from clubs like these.

"Coventry looks pleased with himself," someone muttered beside James. To his left he saw his friend Pierce Chamberlain, the Earl of Wainthorpe.

"Wainthorpe, I didn't expect to see you tonight. I thought you were among those lucky enough to be basking in marital bliss."

Wainthorpe cracked a smile, which lightened the small scar of his temple. "I will agree to the bliss, but if you dare breathe a word to anyone..." Wainthorpe growled.

James chuckled at his friend's reaction. Wainthorpe acted rough but was one of the most softhearted men James had ever met.

"Your secret is safe with me," James promised. "What did you mean about Coventry?"

Wainthorpe crossed his arms and scowled. "Every time one of us gets leg-shackled, he starts grinning from ear to ear as though he played some part in our marriage or is somehow profiting from it. Damned odd."

For a moment neither man spoke. "What brings you here tonight, Pembroke?"

"Trying to drown my sorrows," James replied sardonically, but bitterness clung to his words because they were true. Earlier that day he had met the most wonderful woman and then promptly *lost* her. Gillian Beaumont was a complete mystery to him, and he feared he might never see her again.

"Oh Lord, come and have a drink with me and tell me all about it. As a married man, I can offer solid advice on the fairer sex. None of it will be worth a halfpenny, though."

Wainthorpe's teasing made James smirk again. They took two chairs at a table far enough away from the men playing cards that they could speak without being distracted by the games. A bottle of scotch sat on a silver tray with several glasses, and Wainthorpe poured them both a healthy amount of the drink. They clinked their glasses in a toast, and each took a sip.

"So let's hear about your sorrows."

James sighed. "I met a woman today at a modiste's shop. I was with my sister, Letty, and we made the acquaintance of Miss Gillian Beaumont. You don't happen to know her, do you?" He'd spent all evening asking everyone he knew if the name was familiar, and so far no one had given him any positive responses.

"Beaumont?" Wainthorpe rolled the name over on his tongue, tasting it. "I knew a man named Beaumont, the Earl of Morrey. His son, Adam, is now carrying the title. Decent fellow. His sister is quite lovely, but her name is Caroline. Not Gillian."

"A distant cousin, perhaps?" James wondered aloud.

"Perhaps." Wainthorpe poured himself another drink.

"I could put my cousins on the matter. They're quite good at tracking ladies down."

James snorted. "Lord save anyone who tried to hide from your formidable but lovely cousins." James hastened to add the last bit lest he upset his friend.

"So the woman has you tied in knots, you say?"

"Yes." *Tied in knots* was the right way to put it. After stealing a few kisses in a bookshop, he could still feel her lips against his own like a phantom presence, and her sweet taste still haunted him. Had finding her been simply a matter of curiosity driven by lust, that would have been one thing, but he had a dreadful feeling that she was in grave danger. And he couldn't bear the thought of that, not if it was in his power to protect her.

Earlier that evening, he'd escorted her home after she'd received a letter at Gunter's. When he'd let her out of the coach, she'd been attacked by a lowly coward of a man and rendered unconscious, and the letter she'd received had been stolen. When James had pressed her for details, she'd refused to share anything with him. He'd had no choice but to drop her off at the townhouse of a friend, Viscount Sheridan, and then she'd vanished. He intended to seek out Cedric Sheridan tomorrow and ask who his mysterious guest was and why she might be in danger.

"Well, you can begin your quest tomorrow, eh? You don't want to be out on the streets tonight. Gerald Langley, the one from the Lady Society column, is meeting with that hellfire club he runs. Sometimes that lot gets a bit unruly and takes to the streets. Anyone in their path can find themselves in danger. They almost killed a man a few months ago. They were ready to throw him in the Thames until the Bow Street Runners came upon the scene."

"What? That's awful!" James remembered reading something about that Langley fellow. The man had made a wager with... James's blood froze in his veins. Langley had made a hefty wager to anyone who would seduce a lady named Alexandra Rockford.

James's friend Ambrose Worthing had taken up the wager, but only in order to spare the lady, and he'd later confessed his involvement in the Lady Society column. That column had irreparably damaged Langley's name. Langley had been spreading rumors around town that he would not only unmask Lady Society but do her harm as well.

And today, Ambrose Worthing had given Gillian a note that had resulted in her being attacked. *Surely she...can't be Lady Society?*

"Where does Langley's hellfire club meet?" James demanded, praying Wainthorpe would know.

"On the Strand, or so I hear. Nasty devils. Langley likes to lure virgins to the meetings with promises of finding wealthy husbands, and well, you know..." Wainthorpe didn't finish, but his dark scowl told James everything he needed to know.

James leapt from his chair. "I've got to go. Thank you for the drink."

"Where are you going?" Wainthorpe stood with him, worry knitting his brows.

"To stop Langley. I have a suspicion my mysterious Miss Beaumont might be Lady Society."

"What?" Wainthorpe gaped. "Do you need me to come with you?"

"No, go home to Bianca. Lord knows what mess tonight will bring. I don't want to risk your reputation, and I suspect bringing others might put me in more danger, not less." James smiled at him.

"Send word if you need me," Wainthorpe called out as James left the club.

James hailed a hackney as he rushed down the steps of the club and into the street, telling the driver to take him to the Strand. He only prayed he wouldn't be too late.

As James reached the Strand, he scanned the darkened streets and buildings. Fear for Gillian built inside him like a storm catching on the winds. She was a gently bred lady who shouldn't have to face the horrors of a hellfire club, especially if they learned she was Lady Society. While he trusted she was quite capable of taking care of herself, he was afraid that she was walking into a trap and didn't know it. He had to find her before something happened to her.

With luck, she wouldn't be here, and he would spend the rest of the night watching some fools pretend to throw a black mass and worship the devil. He prayed fervently it was the latter.

He caught a glimpse of a man in a black cloak and a mask walking down the street. He was undoubtedly a hell-fire member. The man paused, glancing about before he headed up the steps to one of the rather unremarkable buildings on the street.

James flung a few coins at his driver and bolted after the figure. He caught up with him just as he was about to lift the knocker. There was only one way inside he could think of, and he had no regrets about his course of action.

"Pardon me," James said.

The man spun to face him, startled. "What the—"

James's fist caught him square on the jaw. The man dropped like a stone and went silent. James dragged the man back down the steps and tucked him behind some bushes planted near the entrance. He slipped the domino off the man's face and pulled it down over his own head and took the cape and fastened it around his shoulders.

He pounded a fist on the door, not even bothering with the knocker. James's heart thundered as he waited, the silence of the street drowning him with its dull roar. After what felt like an eternity, a man answered, a butler from the looks of him, but he seemed far too arrogant, with a hawkish nose and beetle-black eyes that stared at James.

"Yes?"

"I'm here...for the feast." James prayed he was close to whatever nonsense these men were involved with. The butler studied him for a long moment. James stood, silently praying that the butler wouldn't realize he wasn't a real member of the club.

"Ah, you must be the Lord of the Undead. You are late.

The others are sitting down at the feast. The ladies have arrived, and you don't want to miss the festivities."

Lord of the Undead? James didn't know whether to laugh or cringe at the title.

"Very good," James muttered and entered the house. The butler was watching him carefully, and he waited for the man to indicate where he should go.

"Well don't stand there!" he barked. "Show me to the room."

The harsh words deflated the man's arrogance. He snapped to attention and gestured for James to follow him down the hall.

"Apologies, my lord. I assumed you knew the way."

"I was drunk the last time I was here. How can I remember?" Being deep in one's cups was always a decent excuse for not knowing what had happened at a previous engagement. And unshakable confidence had a way of preventing unwanted questions.

The butler's face was still ruddy as he opened the door into the appointed room. There was a large table, and a dozen men were sitting down, drinking. At least six or seven empty bottles of wine were toppled over. The candles were burning low, and shadows played on the walls and the faces of the masked men as they drank and talked. The table was set for dinner, but no food as yet had been served.

James's entrance went unnoticed, and he carefully slid down the side of the room, blending into the group of men. He stole an empty goblet from the table and filled it with wine, feigning a sip as some men laughed in the midst of a bawdy story.

"So I tell the chit she ought to polish my pole, and she says, 'What pole?' And so I showed her, and damned if she didn't faint!" The men burst out laughing. Someone slapped James's shoulder, so he smiled, baring his teeth in a subtle warning. But no one seemed to notice that he wasn't one of them. The domino masks the men wore offered a decent amount of concealment, and he was grateful for that. The last thing he needed was to be associated with these bastards. This was all a pathetic excuse for them to explore their darker sides at the risk of destroying innocence.

"Gentlemen!" A man's booming voice called the stories and laughter to a halt. Everyone, including James, turned to face the man who stood at the head of the long dining table. The fire in the white marble fireplace behind him snapped and cracked, and the light from the flames created an eerie silhouette of the speaker.

"Tonight, we have a feast prepared. As I mentioned at our previous meeting, we have several *special* guests, some ladies with whom you are well acquainted. They wish once more to participate in the dark arts, and we have two delicious young virgin beauties who graciously volunteered to sate our need for the blood of the innocent."

There were cruel snickers, laughter, and muttered jokes about taking maidenheads. James clenched his fists.

If he lost control, he might very well strangle someone. A woman's innocence was no laughing matter, and he was quite certain, whoever these beauties were, they didn't know they were about to be cast into the lions' den.

"Are you prepared?" the man at the head of the table asked. The lords in the room burst into loud, obnoxious cheering and whistling. The dining room door opened, and six ladies entered the room. They were followed by a man who closed the doors behind them, sealing everyone inside. The ladies were escorted to the remaining empty chairs at the table.

"My friends, as the Lord of Lust, let me present our guests to you." The so-called Lord of Lust began to name each lady. James studied the buxom and beautiful ladies beneath their half masks, each one smiling coquettishly as her name was called. The Lady of Sin, the Lady of the Night, the Lady of Dark Desire...and so on. But the Lord of Lust paused when he got to the last two.

There was a woman wearing a red gown and another in a purple gown, and despite the masks they wore, neither seemed all that excited to be present at the feast, given their frowns. In fact, both of them looked quite frightened, by the way their hands were white-knuckled into fists and their faces pale below their masks.

James recognized the purple gown with a wave of dread. It was the same gown he'd seen Gillian buying in the shop earlier that day. The image of her in the changing area wearing that dress as he'd caught a glimpse of her still haunted him in a bittersweet way. He couldn't forget the vulnerable pools of her gray eyes or the way her lips had parted when she'd realized he was staring at her only partially clothed.

His worst fear had come true. Gillian Beaumont—*his* beautiful, mysterious Gillian—was seated at a table with the worst sort of men all around her, men who wanted a chance to force her to have intercourse.

Over my dead body, he vowed.

"Now, last but not least, we have a most esteemed guest amongst us. You recall the scathing, poisonous pen of that bitch queen who calls herself Lady Society?" the Lord of Lust spat. The men around him harrumphed, and a few pounded their fists on the table. Gillian and the other lady jumped a little in their seats.

"Well, tonight I set the perfect trap and lured Lady Society herself to my door. I let it slip at a ball the other evening that we would be meeting tonight and that she wouldn't want to miss our entertainment." The Lord of Lust prowled slowly down the room to the woman in the red dress and the woman in the purple dress. "But which is Lady Society, I wonder?" he mused aloud. "I suppose it doesn't matter. We will have the pleasure of having both of you." He snapped his fingers, and the men on either side of the ladies suddenly grabbed their arms, jerking them behind the chairs and winding ropes around their wrists.

"How dare you, Mr. Langley!" the woman in the red dress exclaimed with a violent gnash of her white teeth, like a badger bent on attacking. "I'll do more than write a bloody article destroying you. I'll have your bollocks on a silver platter!" Where had he heard that voice before?

God's teeth! The little spitfire was Viscount Sheridan's younger sister, Audrey Sheridan. What was *she* doing here? He glanced at Gillian, who was biting her lip and jerking at the bonds, trying to free herself.

"How dare I? My dear lady," the Lord of Lust growled, "you came here of your own free will. No one forced you here. I daresay there are few who would have any sympathy for a woman who *willingly* went to a hellfire club. Your reputation will be worthless, and your word unfit for print. And that's only the beginning of what I have planned for you tonight. You wrecked my family, my name—everything! And I will destroy you for it!"

"You got only what you deserved, you bastard!" Audrey snarled with surprising ferocity for such a tiny, soft-looking little woman.

"And you have the mouth of a whore," the lord growled. "I plan to treat you like one."

The two women gaped in horror. James gripped the arms of his chair in a white-knuckled hold. He had to think of a plan, one that wouldn't risk the two ladies. He was not averse to a good brawl, but he didn't like the odds against him.

"Gag them. I wish for silence while we enjoy our feast." The Lord of Lust snapped his fingers, and the men on either side of Audrey and Gillian stuffed handkerchiefs into the girls' mouths, drowning out the threats Audrey tried to hurl.

James now noted that Audrey had called the Lord of Lust Langley. Wainthorpe had been right—the devilish leader of this band of fools was Gerald Langley. The foul, odious man who'd given Ambrose Worthing and his beloved wife of his so much trouble. It was clear from the crazed look in Langley's eyes that he was unhinged. What-ever James did tonight to help Audrey, Gillian would be that much more endangered. Langley wouldn't let them simply stroll out of there unharmed, not when Audrey and Gillian had made tonight's festivities so personal to the man. He wanted blood, possibly even a life, if she couldn't keep her temper in check.

"Now," Langley said with a chuckle. "I'm famished." He picked up a bell by the end of the table and rang it. A moment later several footmen entered, bringing trays with the first course.

"My lord, what about...?" One of the men pointed to the single empty chair left at the table.

"Oh, right." Langley sighed with boredom and nodded at one the nearest footmen. "Bring in His Unholiness."

James tensed, wondering what new horror these men would create, but he almost laughed out loud when the footman returned with a large handsome black cat and placed the creature on the table, offering it a plate of food. The cat hunched down, his yellow eyes taking in every single person in the room before he cautiously bent his head to his plate and began to pick at the offering.

"Pleased to meet our guest, Lady Society? He's the oldest member, you see," Langley said solemnly. "*Ancient* you might say."

Ancient? James tilted his head, and then it hit him. His Unholiness...ancient... Langley and his pack of crazed followers believed that the cat was the devil himself? *Good God.* This was worse than he feared. The men weren't out simply to drink and copulate and feign at devil worship—they believed it. They were truly mad.

James continued to play along, picking at the food that was brought to him, but he couldn't keep his eyes off Gillian. Her face was ashen, and she barely moved, except the tiny tensing of her bared arms. She seemed to be fighting her bonds, quietly, carefully. So far no one else seemed to notice. Smart creature she was, very smart, and for that he was thankful. She would stay calm if things got complicated, which they almost certainly would. James took another drink of wine from his goblet, only half listening to the men around him boasting of how they planned to enjoy the evening.

The women, aside from Audrey and Gillian, were quite willing and familiar with the members of the club, which meant James didn't need to add them to the list of damsels in need of rescuing. He almost smiled. Earlier that day when he'd been trying to rescue Gillian from a man who'd attacked her to get a letter warning her about tonight, she had told him most emphatically that she was not a damsel in need of rescuing.

One of the men close to Langley drew his attention away from Gillian. He was toying with his fork, scowling, his gaze darting down the length of the table toward where the two ladies were being held. The man's face was partially hidden behind a domino mask, like his own, yet his sandy blond hair and green eyes were familiar. The man didn't eat or drink like the rest, and his eyes kept focusing back on the two women. Rather than appearing like a man ready to prey upon the ladies, he looked...

James caught the man's gaze, and the man's eyes bored into his. He saw shock and recognition there, which was returned in kind. He knew now how he knew this man.

There was only one person of his acquaintance who fit the man's profile. Jonathan St. Laurent. The younger half brother of the infamous Duke of Essex, one of James's friends, was a member of this club? He'd rather liked the man, but if it turned out he was a party to these dark deeds, James would throttle him.

As the feast drew to a close, Langley stood, drew out a pair of dice from a coat pocket, and held them up.

"Each man shall toss the sacred dice to determine who gets the joy of bedding the one in the purple gown. Then we will cast the die for Lady Society. But rest assured we have all night, and every man gets a chance with *both* ladies."

Audrey rocked wildly in her chair, her shouts muffled by her gag.

James glanced back at Jonathan and saw a flash of furious fire in the man's eyes. Perhaps he was mistaken. Perhaps St. Laurent was here like him, to help?

The dice were passed around, each man rolling them, then cursing or whooping as the numbers fell onto the table. If James could win the highest number for Gillian, he might be able to get her to safety and come back for Audrey. If he had to fight, one lady would be easier to shield than two.

When the dice were handed to him, he held his breath and got to his feet. He met Gillian's gaze, wishing that she knew he was there, that she wasn't facing this horror alone. He flung the dice down the length of the table and closed his eyes for a brief instant until the sound of the dice clattering against the wood ceased.

"Twelve!" the man roared. "By God, you're a lucky bastard!" The man next to him slapped him hard on the arm.

"It seems we have our winner." Langley smiled at him. "Take your pretty prize to any of the upstairs rooms. I'll give you half an hour, and then we shall roll to see who is next."

James drew in his breath slowly, his head spinning a little. He was at least going to be able to get Gillian out of here. He smiled at the men around him, pretending to enjoy the congratulations as he walked to claim Gillian.

the wall. James cursed as he saw Gillian's head strike the wall, and she crumpled to the ground. He rushed toward her, but a deep bellowing shout stopped him in his tracks.

"Halt or I will put a bullet in your back!" Langley's threat was followed by a pistol barrel digging between his shoulder blades.

James breathed out slowly, staring at Gillian, who was getting to her knees, clutching a hand to her head. That was two blows today—blows that would have felled a bigger man than his tiny sweet Gillian. Behind him, he heard the scuffle and crashes of men fighting in the dining room. St. Laurent must be using his fists now. James almost smiled. Anyone facing that man's bared hands wouldn't be standing for long. He'd trained with the best.

"Wait...I know you. So how does the Earl of Pembroke find his way into my little club without an invitation?" Langley demanded.

"A terrible lack of security, for one."

Langley jammed the barrel into the back of his neck this time. "Shut up!"

James had only seconds to act, only one chance to move the right way. He jerked to the right, and the barrel slid off his neck as he crouched and spun, grappling with Langley. The pistol fired, but the bullet lodged in the ceiling, sending a shower of plaster down around him and Langley.

James roared and tackled Langley to the ground and

wrestled the gun from his hands. Langley's mask fell off during the struggle, his wild eyes glittering dangerously.

"I'll not stand for this! You cannot break into my club—"

James punched him in the face, and he fell back on the floor, his eyes rolling back in his head.

"I did, and I would do it again, you bastard," James muttered.

James looked up, peering through the half-open dining room doors. All he saw was Audrey clutching a screeching black cat and Jonathan throwing punches in every direction. Audrey sought him, her face frantic.

"Lord Pembroke! Heavens! I'm so glad to see you! Where's Gillian?"

He waved hastily behind him, before he turned back to Gillian. She was sitting back against the wall, her head in her hands, blood dripping down her cheek, and he realized to his horror that part of the ceiling had fallen on her.

"Miss Beaumont..." He knelt beside her, cupping her face in his hands and turning her wounded side into the light of the candles in the wall sconces above.

"My lord...I do not feel well," she said drowsily.

"I know, sweetheart, I know." He grimaced as he examined her. She needed to be seen by a doctor immediately.

"Wait here. Miss Sheridan and St. Laurent require assistance." He hated to leave her, but Jonathan couldn't hope to fend off all those cads by himself. Once he was certain the other man was all right, he'd go straight back to Gillian.

"Go. I'll be fine," she promised him. James leaned in and brushed a swift kiss over her lips before he ran into the fray in the dining room.

Everything seemed to be a bit hazy. Gillian watched James explode into the dining room. He moved with a surprising swiftness and ease, as if he was quite accustomed to battling the minions of a hellfire club. Earlier that day he had shown her his sweet, irresistible, and all too seductive side, but now she saw a warrior before her.

She tried to walk toward him but tripped. Her feet felt clumsy, and she looked down. She blinked past the pain in her head, and with an odd distant feeling she noticed that the beautiful purple gown she wore was torn, and—was that blood smeared on her bodice? *Heavens...whose blood is that?* The sound of fighting drew her attention back to the dining room, and she looked up.

Her mouth fell open as she saw James grab a man and throw him over the table as he fought his way to Jonathan.

Audrey stood in the corner of the dining room, a black cat in her arms and a fireplace poker in one hand. She faced a drunken lout who was stumbling toward her. Audrey wielded the poker like a fencing master would face an opponent. She swung hard and knocked the man down with a swift blow. Then she faced the hallway, still holding the feline under one arm. *What the devil is Audrey doing with a cat and—*

"Gillian?" Audrey shouted when she saw Gillian sitting in the hall. "Are you all right?"

"Y-yes." Gillian stumbled toward her, and that's when she felt the stickiness dripping down her cheek. She reached up and touched her face. Her hand came back covered in blood. The sight of the scarlet liquid on her palm made her flinch. *She* was the one bleeding?

She glanced back at her mistress in time to see Jonathan help Audrey and the cat through an open windowsill. They vanished into the night. Suddenly James appeared, catching her by the hand.

"Time to go. Can you run?"

"I think so," she said, glad he was pulling her along because it seemed she might not have the strength after all.

"Why did they go out the window?" she asked as she and James rushed down the corridor. The path that led back to the dining room was blocked as men were coming fast behind her and James, but as of yet they hadn't been spotted.

"They had a chance to get out that way. It's better if we split up so that we can hide easier in the shadows and attract less attention. I know of another way out. Many of these old houses are based on the same floor plans—" James paused at the end of the hall and shoved the door open hard enough that it crashed against the wall. They stumbled into the kitchens, where a surly looking woman with a greasy apron stared at them.

"Oi! What are you doing here?" the cook demanded.

James didn't bother to answer; he simply headed straight for the door at the end of the kitchens. Gillian followed, dodging pots and coughing as steam filled her lungs. They burst outside into a darkened alleyway, and James hastily led her to the street, where he hailed a hackney that was passing by. He shouted an address to the driver.

"And another ten shillings if you get us the hell off this bloody street," he added.

"That I can do!" the old driver said.

James lifted Gillian into the coach and set her down gently in the seat facing away from the driver. The coach jerked into motion, and she fell against James. He caught her, keeping her from toppling to the floor.

"I've got you," he said. The words seem to resonate deeply with her, even more than the simple act of catching her. The evening had been a complete blur, and yet having him hold her seemed to ground her. Only now was she able to finally catch her breath.

"My lord, what were you doing there?" Gillian reached up to touch her aching head.

"I was rescuing you—not that I did a very good job of it. Careful," he said as he grasped her hand and gently pulled it away from her temple. "You're bleeding."

"I really didn't need to be rescued," she reminded him, though she was fully aware of just how ludicrous that sounded given the situation she'd found herself in.

Chasing after her mistress into a hellfire club—into a trap, no less—was not one of her brighter moments, and she despised her own foolishness. If there was one thing she could have claimed proudly, it was that she knew how to be responsible and sensible. Nothing about tonight had been sensible. Instead, she had been reckless and almost lost her life. When she glanced James's way, she saw him biting his lip rather than arguing with her.

"You are right," she grumbled. "I was in trouble. Thank you for coming to my aid."

He smiled warmly, and it brought back a fresh wave of memories from earlier that day, how he'd teased her in the library and kissed her senseless. She had let him believe she wasn't a lady's maid, but an actual lady. She couldn't hide the truth from him anymore. He'd saved her life, and she owed him her honesty.

"My lord..." she began, but the coach stopped, and the driver announced the address. This was not the Sheridan townhouse. "Where are we?"

James looked at his boots then, suddenly bashful. "I

brought you to my home. It's late, so no one will see you. I have a doctor who lives with me because of my mother, and I want him to look at you at once. The moment he has assured me that you are well, I will escort you wherever you wish."

His mother? She struggled to remember what James's sister, Letty, had said to her. James's mother had fallen ill after their father had died and over the last two years had become withdrawn and forgetful. Knowing that he looked after his mother filled Gillian with a sense of sympathetic compassion.

"Is that acceptable? Taking you home?" His voice was soft, silken, though a little dangerous in the way it made her heart flutter. He was exactly the sort of man she had dreamed of falling in love with. But she never could. He was a titled peer, a member of the *haute ton*. She was an earl's bastard daughter.

If I dared to dream, you would be mine.

She couldn't look away from him as she nodded. She shouldn't agree to go into his house, but she longed for one moment to pretend that this life might have been hers. Part of her heart still clung to foolish girlhood dreams, wanted to believe for one night that she was a highborn lady who could be seen with him, who could marry him, who could have a life with him.

He climbed out of the coach and held out his hand to her. She started to exit the vehicle, and he gripped her by the waist carefully, slowly letting her slide down his body

being damaged, it was him. She was the undesirable one here.

"My lord, I really must speak with you," she said softly, knowing she had to tell him the truth about her station.

"I want Dr. Wilkes to see you first. Then you can tell me whatever it is you wish to tell me."

She leaned back in the chair by the fireplace and watched him pace the floor. Had her head not been pounding she would have chuckled at seeing him so clearly vexed over her when he really ought not to be worried. She would be fine.

"You must be careful not to wear a path into the rugs," she said, finally letting a smile slip at his fretfulness. The man was a worrier. Her amusement faded as she realized it must have come from him becoming an earl so young and bearing his mother's illness and his sister's welfare as his own responsibility.

"Hmm?" he responded before he realized what she'd said. With a wry chuckle, he stopped. "Yes, wouldn't want to wear down the carpets."

His lips parted again as though he was about to speak, but the door opened and a kindly looking middle-aged gentleman entered. He wore breeches and a shirt, but no waistcoat.

"My apologies, my lord, for my state of undress. But Brandon informed me that a lady here is in distress?"

"Yes. Dr. Wilkes, this is Miss Gillian Beaumont. Miss Beaumont, this is Dr. Giles Wilkes."

"Pleased to meet you," Gillian said.

"And you as well." Wilkes smiled as he approached her. "Let's have a look, shall we? The head, is it?"

James moved beside her, frowning in the most darling way while Dr. Wilkes examined her eyes, head, and neck.

"I need to cleanse the wound and see exactly how deep the damage goes. Miss Beaumont, can I persuade you to sit on the bed?"

"Of course." Gillian sat on the bed and tried to hold still as Dr. Wilkes retrieved several items from his black medicine bag.

Dr. Wilkes took his time examining her and instructed James to hold a candelabra closer so he had proper lighting.

"Do you mind if I inquire as to how you were injured, Miss Beaumont?"

"Well, I was shoved hard against a wall, and I think part of the ceiling fell down on top of me."

Wilkes gaped at her and then at James. "Pardon?"

"It's a long story, but I was helping her escape a hellfire club. Things became complicated."

"I see." Dr. Wilkes frowned as he used a mixture of witch hazel to clean her scrapes. Gillian hissed at the sting, but James's powerful hand gripped one of hers as he stood beside her next to the bed, which comforted her somewhat.

"She should not be left alone tonight. The wound appears to be superficial, but she should be watched closely in case she's having any pain. I want to be woken at once if that's the case."

"Oh, but I cannot stay—" Gillian protested.

"You can and you will." James squeezed her hand again. "If Dr. Wilkes is concerned about you, you must do what he says."

"But...I have no clothes, and Miss Sheridan will worry about where I am."

It was dangerous to stay. She would be too close to the man who tempted her like no other had.

"I will send a messenger to Miss Sheridan at once. I'm sure Letty will have some extra clothes you can borrow." James caught her chin, turning Gillian's head to face him. "Please, let me take care of you." Their eyes locked, and she had that feeling that his words weren't simply about tonight, but for many nights to come.

He doesn't even know who I am. If he did, he would be furious at my deception.

"Are you comfortable with that, Miss Beaumont?" Dr. Wilkes asked.

What could she say? "If it is what you recommend, then yes."

"I'll stay to watch over you, if you have no objection." James still held her hand, and heat crept into her cheeks at the thought of him being so close to her while she slept.

"I don't," she said, unable to tear her gaze away from his eyes. They were warm and soft, a shade of brown that made her think of cinnamon.

"Good." James let go of her hand, and then he walked with the doctor to the hallway.

Gillian curled her arms around her waist. She knew that what she was doing was wrong. Staying here with him was scandalous. She'd told him not to worry about her reputation, because she was afraid he'd try to do the honorable thing and offer marriage, and then he'd despise her once he learned the truth of her situation. A woman in service lived and died by her reputation, and while Audrey might not care about this level of scandal, it would spread and make the Sheridan house lose respect, which would hurt Audrey. Gillian felt like Audrey was her closest friend, even though they were employer and employee.

The door opened a little while later to reveal James and a young maid. The woman held a nightgown and other necessities in her arms.

"Miss Beaumont, this is Sybil. She'll see to your needs. I'll give you half an hour to see that you're settled." He paused by the door. The uncertain, almost worried look on his face was strangely charming, as if he feared to leave her alone in case she might need him.

"Thank you, my lord. I will be fine until you return," she promised.

Sybil helped her change out of the dark purple dress and into the nightgown. The expensive fabric made her feel embarrassed. Did it belong to James's sister, Letty? The fine lace at her throat and breasts was too lovely, too expensive compared to the simple homespun cotton gown she always wore. It had to belong to his sister.

"Do you need anything else, miss?" Sybil asked. She finished taking down Gillian's hair from the hasty coiffure she'd styled earlier that evening. She'd had to rush from the house after Audrey and only had time for a simple chignon. Many of the pins had become tangled during her earlier struggles, but the maid had a talent for setting them free.

"No, I'm quite all right, thank you." It was odd to be on the receiving end of help like this. She'd spent most of her life taking care of herself and Audrey in much the same way.

"If you need anything else, just use the bell cord by the bed. We always have some staff remain awake at night because—" The maid suddenly covered her mouth. "I shouldn't have spoken, miss. It's not my place to—"

"It's all right, Sybil. I'm sure it has to do with Lord Pembroke's mother and her illness."

The maid bit her lip and nodded. Gillian thanked her again and pulled back the coverlet and the bedclothes before she climbed into bed.

She blew out the candle by her head and snuggled down into the soft feather mattress. It was far better than the slender cot she slept on in the attic of the Sheridan townhouse. Her accommodations at home were better than many ladies in service, but nothing could compare to a fine mattress like this. She closed her eyes, smiling a little.

"Feeling better?"

She jolted up at the sound of James's voice. He had slipped into the room silently, holding a book and a candlestick.

"Yes." She brushed her hair back from her face and watched him as he closed the bedroom door and walked over to a chair by the fireplace.

"Good. I didn't mean to wake you. Please, rest. I'll be here if you need me." He waved the book in his hand, then settled into a chair by the fire. Gillian wondered if his broad shoulders ever tired of the burdens he carried. He bore so much responsibility, and she couldn't help but feel sorrow at the knowledge that there was no one to care for him.

She was still a bit shocked that she was sleeping at the Earl of Pembroke's house and he was in her bedchamber. Despite her weariness, her nerves sprang to life, and she knew she wouldn't get to sleep anytime soon. She slipped out of bed, went over to the chair beside him, and eased herself into the seat. He glanced up in surprise.

"I can't sleep. Not yet. Would you read to me?"

He looked down at the book in his hands, and a lock of his dark hair fell over his eyes. She couldn't take her gaze off his face, the way the firelight shadowed the elegant ridges of his jaw and cheekbones. His features had been crafted by the goddess of love to tempt any sane woman into thinking scandalous thoughts. Gillian remembered how soft those lips were, how they'd felt teasing hers, the wicked flick of his tongue sending delicious shivers down her spine.

"You wish for me to read to you?" He raised the book so she might see the spine, which was embossed *Lady Gloria and the Earnest Earl*. "Are you quite sure?" His voice was low, a seductive glint in his eyes, but there was humor twitching at the corners of his lips. "After all, the last time I read to you..." His gaze lowered to her lips as he paused, and then he met her eyes. "We got quite lost, as I recall, and not in the pages." She flushed as she realized he could somehow tease her and arouse her passions at the same time.

"I believe I'm willing to risk getting lost again—in the pages, I mean." She had a feeling this man could read anything to her and she would cling to his every word and syllable. She bit her lip to keep from laughing at herself.

James opened the book again, leaning toward her in his chair as he turned back to the first page.

"Best to start at the beginning, I think."

Gillian tucked her legs up in her chair and leaned on the left arm to get comfortable. The warmth of the fire and the heat between her and James filled the room, making her feel soft, feminine, and all too aware of him as a man in a way that made her head dizzy for completely different reasons.

"'It always seems that when a lady most needs adventure, such an adventure comes knocking upon her door. For Miss Gloria Bellarmy, the knock was indeed an actual knock upon her door, in the form of a tall, dark stranger in need of help.'" James continued to read the Gothic novel, his deep voice pronouncing the words in a seductive tone and sending Gillian into a tranquil mood.

She closed her eyes, picturing the scenes of the book. But rather than Miss Gloria as the heroine, it was she who was accompanying the mysterious man to his beautiful but crumbling home off the coast of Cornwall. And it was James who seduced her in the dining room, who carried her off to bed and made love to her with a savage intensity that aroused rather than frightened her. The dreams were exquisite. She almost whimpered in protest when her body was suddenly lifted off the chair, and she came awake in James's arms.

"You were asleep," he whispered huskily. "I thought I ought to take you to bed."

"Take me to bed?" she murmured, her body humming at the thought. Gillian looked up to his face and slowly curled her arms around his neck as he carried her to the bed.

"Yes, you need rest." He set her down, but when she didn't let go, he stayed hovering over her. Their faces were inches apart in the candlelight.

"Gillian." His voice was rougher now. He was on the edge, and she could feel it too. The invisible edge that if they crossed they would fall into scandal and sin, but did it really matter? The hunger she had for him outweighed the rational thoughts she had clung to earlier.

"Would it be so bad to—" She didn't finish the thought but simply lowered her gaze to his tempting mouth. *Lord, please let him kiss me.* She trembled in his arms with the force of her hunger for him.

"It would be very bad...and *very good.*" He braced one arm on the other side of her as he leaned even farther over the bed. "But I promised I would be a gentleman."

Gillian's body was already humming at the thought of him kissing her again. There was something about him that deprived her of good sense. A gentleman who had a wild side, a gentleman who loved deeply and fought madly to protect those he cared about, including her.

Damn the consequences. She moved one of her hands to his cravat, tugging at the white neckcloth, unraveling it until it was loose enough to slide off him. She let it drop to the floor. He glanced at it, and when he looked up at her again, his luscious lips split into a wonderfully wicked grin. Sparks shot down her body as she reached for the buttons of his waistcoat at the same time he reached for her night-gown at her waist. They both laughed softly, their faces brushing cheek to cheek as they rushed to remove the other's clothing. It was as though Gillian's natural self-consciousness had faded into the night, and all that remained was a creature of touch, taste, and scent as she explored each bit of James's body with her hands and mouth as she undressed him.

By the time he'd been stripped of his clothes, he was lifting her nightgown over her head. She didn't have any time to be shy. He was crawling on top of her, kissing her madly.

"Open for me, love," he whispered against her lips. She opened her mouth, but he gave a gentle tap on her knees, and she tensed.

"Easy now," he said with a chuckle. "We'll go slow." James nuzzled her cheek, and she clutched his shoulders as she slowly opened herself to him. The heavy weight of his body was welcome; it made her feel grounded like an ancient tree in a wild forgotten garden that was growing deep roots to the center of the earth itself. That was how bonded, how connected he made her feel to him.

They seemed to kiss for hours, the gentle urging lips, the questing hands and sliding limbs as they explored each other. She'd never felt such a slow building need inside her before, one that seemed to exist outside of her as she sought something greater.

"Is it always like this?" she asked against his lips.

"Like what?" he replied, his tone husky.

She raked her fingers through his hair at the nape of his neck, and he shuddered. "Like...like I'm on fire all over, like I need you in a way I barely understand." She would have blushed at her own openness, but in that moment, she didn't care.

"No, it isn't always like this. I feel the same," he admitted, a boyish smile on his face rendering her speechless. Lost for words, Gillian kissed his chin, his throat, digging her nails into his shoulders as he slowly entered her. The tightness, the hint of pain flashed inside her womb like a shooting star and then faded into a sensation of fullness. He completed her in that moment, made her whole in a way she'd never imagined. This was the reason women fell in love, the reason why rakes were so dangerous. James wasn't a rake. He was a gentleman, just as he'd promised. But he was a gentleman who knew how to use his body in the most wonderfully wicked ways.

"Move with me," he encouraged between kisses. Gillian raised her hips as he lowered his, and the sensation of fullness increased until she almost couldn't breathe. Then he withdrew, and she gripped him harder, urging him to thrust back in. They shared a soft moan as their hips came together over and over.

"You feel like heaven," he growled. "Bloody heaven."

"So do you." Gillian gasped as he thrust back into her, and a wave of pleasure suddenly and frighteningly swept over her.

She inhaled and cried out. A second later James covered her mouth with his, muffling her cries. Then he thrust into her again and buried his face in her neck, kissing her softly as he collapsed on top of her. For a moment, she feared she couldn't breathe, but he lifted his body and rolled to the side. Gillian's bare body started to cool, and for a second reason and logic threatened to sweep her away, but James lifted the covers over them and pulled her into his arms, kissing the shell of her ear.

"Sleep. I'm here to watch over you." His promise followed her into the darkness as sleep closed in at last.

JAMES HELD GILLIAN IN HIS ARMS, WATCHING THE candles slowly burn down. He had been reckless, taking her like that, and yet he did not regret an instant. She was the woman he wanted to spend the rest of his life with, but he knew he was going to have trouble convincing her to marry him. There were secrets in her eyes and sorrow upon her lips, and he wished he knew what it was that filled her with fear and hesitancy. He lived his entire life feeling distanced and alone from others. It was hard to find a young lady in society who would marry a man who wished to keep his mother close, a mother who suffered from an early onset of an illness of the mind. Many young ladies he had met had mentioned they would wish to see his mother retired to the country, out of sight, out of mind, but James couldn't do that. Gillian seemed to understand him and had compassion like no other woman he'd met. She was the sort of woman he could marry.

He brushed a stray lock of hair back from her face, and she snuggled closer to him. The light floral scent that clung to her hair made him think of those long-ago summers when he was a boy in the country. His father had herself up to him, shared her body with him and he with her.

She had slept with James. No, Lord Pembroke. He could never be James. She was a servant, and he was a lord. He had to be kept in his position and she in hers.

I've made a terrible mistake.

Yet Gillian couldn't deny how wonderful she felt. Her body was sated in a way she'd never imagined, and when she tried to slip out of James's hold her body protested, wanting instead to sink back down in the warm bed with him. She forced herself to move, lifting his arm around her waist and setting it down at his side. He murmured something soft in his sleep and rolled onto his stomach away from her. A sigh of relief escaped her as she slipped out of the bed.

It took a few minutes to collect her things. Her gown was wrinkled and still covered with droplets of blood and white plaster dust, which she did her best to shake off.

"Lord, what a mess," she muttered, then froze as James moved in bed, flipping his pillow before settling back.

Once she was dressed, she peeled back the curtains by the sash window. Dawn was but a faint pink line upon the trees and the tops of the houses of the London streets. She believed she had enough time to find a coach and get home before the Sheridan house awoke to find her gone. Letting Sean Hartley, her friend and footman, know what had happened was one thing, but she did not want the rest of the staff to know her grave mistake.

Biting her lips, she slipped her boots on and laced them up, then crept to the door and eased it open. She slipped into the hall and checked for servants, finding no one. Gillian knew they would be rising any moment. The cook down in the kitchens would be wrapping her apron around her waist and checking on the bread from the night before. Footmen would begin making their rounds lighting lamps, and maids would soon start opening curtains and preparing breakfast trays for James and his family. Gillian knew these routines all too well because it was her world, the world of whispered orders and bells, of tea trays and laundry. Her world was not one of luscious beds, fine gowns, and glittering balls. That was the world James belonged to.

At least I have the memories to keep me warm in the long, lonely years ahead.

Gillian crept down the stairs and reached the front door.

"Miss Beaumont?" Dr. Wilkes's voice froze her in her tracks. She looked over her shoulder and saw the doctor emerge from a downstairs room.

"Oh, good morning, Dr. Wilkes. How are you?"

The doctor smiled. "Well. And how are you feeling? I would like to look at your head before you leave."

"Oh, but..."

"Please," he said. "I am a doctor, and it's my nature to worry. It will only take a moment. I was just seeing to the dowager countess with her morning medicine. She's in the drawing room. If you don't mind, I prefer to keep an eye on her while we are alone."

"Er, yes, of course." Gillian followed him into the drawing room. An older woman was seated in a chair facing the window overlooking a lovely garden. The purple morning light set off in the bright hues of the wisteria climbing the walls around the windows. The woman's hand was splayed on the glass, as if she yearned to touch the colorful blossoms outside.

"How is she?" Gillian asked the doctor.

Dr. Wilkes's voice was full of compassion. "A little more distant today. She has her good days and bad days."

Gillian's throat tightened as she thought of James having to care for his mother on those bad days when she was barely there.

"Now, let's have a look at you." Dr. Wilkes brought her close to the window by James's mother so he could examine her head. "Looks clean, but there's a bit of swelling. It will likely bruise. How do you feel?"

"A little tender is all."

"Any cloudiness or muddy thoughts?"

"No." Her thoughts were scattered, but it had nothing to do with being hit in the head and everything to do with the man who had made love to her.

"Hello," a soft feminine voice said, making Gillian tense until she realized it was James's mother. She was watching Gillian with curious brown eyes.

"Hello," Gillian replied and looked to Dr. Wilkes, who offered an encouraging smile.

"Abigail, this is Miss Gillian Beaumont. She's a friend of James's."

"Oh?" The woman's face lit with a smile. "You know my James?"

"Yes." Gillian tried to ignore the heat rising to her face.

"He's such a good boy, always following his father about. So like my Henry."

Gillian's smile faltered as she realized his mother was thinking of the past as though it were the present. Gillian recovered quickly, adapting.

"What is Henry like?" she asked the older woman.

"Henry?" She smiled dreamily. "He's a perfect gentleman. I married him when I was only seventeen. He was twenty-four and oh so handsome. All my friends were terribly jealous. I didn't care that he was the future Earl of Pembroke, however. To me he was simply Henry. I was only a squire's daughter, you see. I never thought he would even notice me, but, well, I was a wonderful dancer. The best men love to dance as much as we women do."

Gillian sat down in a chair beside the dowager countess. "Oh?"

"Yes. I had tiny, quick feet back then." She giggled. "Henry came down from London that year, and we danced at his father's Christmas ball. He told me years later that he never regretted dancing with only me that night, though his parents were quite scandalized."

As Gillian left the house, the sun finally rose over the tops of the other houses, painting the streets with pale morning light. Coaches were beginning to rumble along the cobblestones, and soon people would be taking early walks. Gillian waved down a coach and took one last look back at James's home. Then she bid goodbye to her dreams once and for all.

⚜

SHE WAS GONE. WHEN JAMES WOKE A FEW HOURS AFTER dawn, the realization had been like a knife to his chest. The woman he'd shared the most intimate night with had abandoned him. Rather than James running out like a heartless rogue, she was the one who had fled. It was as though the world had turned upside down on him.

James hunched over on the edge of the bed, staring at the floor where his clothes lay in a crumpled heap. He was completely naked, which wasn't unusual, but for once he felt exposed. He'd never taken mistresses, had only bedded one other woman in his life before last night, but damned if he didn't feel as though he had lost his virginity rather than Gillian losing hers.

"My lord?" Dr. Wilkes's voice came through the closed door.

"Yes, Dr. Wilkes. Give me a moment." He scrambled out of bed and hastily threw on his clothes. When he opened the door, Dr. Wilkes was standing there, frowning.

"I wished to check on you. It's not like you to—" Dr. Wilkes's eyes strayed to the bed and the blood spotting that James had forgotten to cover in his haste to answer the door.

Damn, the man would surely know what had happened.

Dr. Wilkes cleared his throat. "Miss Beaumont has left. When you missed breakfast, I grew worried." Dr. Wilkes, ever the professional, did not mention what he clearly understood had happened last night.

"Is there any food left?" he asked.

"The cook kept a few kippers, herring, and eggs in some chafing dishes on the sideboard. They should still be hot."

"Thank you." James knew he should wash and dress in fresh clothes, but his stomach ached. He hadn't had much in the way of dinner before he'd gone off to Coventry's Wicked Earls' Club.

"How is my mother today?" he asked as the doctor kept pace with him.

"Well enough. Miss Beaumont had the opportunity to meet your mother while I examined her wound before she left."

James froze. Gillian had met his mother? No wonder she had fled the house. Being compassionate with words was easier than being compassionate by deed. No doubt she'd been overwhelmed by his mother's deteriorating condition and fled.

"Was Miss Beaumont very unsettled by my mother?" He tried to keep emotion out of his voice.

"Not at all." Dr. Wilkes and James descended the stairs and headed to the drawing room. "She had a pleasant conversation with her and got her to talk much more than I've been able to in days."

James's heart gave a little start. It was not what he had expected to hear.

"Truly? She was talking to Gillian?"

The doctor eyed him for a moment, perhaps noting that he'd called Gillian by her first name, then answered. "Yes, she spoke about your father and how they met. Always a charming story." Dr. Wilkes's eyes were soft, and it made James proud that he'd found one of the few physicians in London who didn't let science alone rule his head. It was the reason James had hired him. He needed a man who had a heart to care for his mother.

"And Gillian, how is she? I didn't get to see her before she left this morning."

"She seems fine. That woman has a strong, sturdy skull, thank heavens."

As he and Dr. Wilkes entered into the dining room, James collected a plate and helped himself to kippers and eggs and coffee before he took a seat facing the gardens. Dr. Wilkes walked to the window and stared at the view.

"Is my mother resting?" James asked.

"Yes." The doctor turned toward James, still frowning. "My lord, she's beginning to lose control of her limbs, and she's been trying to walk about without the servants to watch for her. I'm worried that if she falls, we won't..." The man's words faded into the silence of the room.

James set his fork down, his stomach knotting painfully. "What do you propose we do?"

The heavy solemnity of the doctor's voice terrified James. "We should think about moving her to the Pembroke estate. I know you wish to stay close to her, but she will need to live in a place without stairs. The manor house has rooms on the first floor."

Dr. Wilkes was right. The estate would be better for her with fewer stairs, but that would mean he would not see her as often. Much of his family's investments kept him busy in London. He thought it over for a long moment. His mother had made so many sacrifices, as all mothers do, and losing their father had been the hardest on her. James wanted to do what was best for her. He owed her the best care for her steadfast love for him and Letty all these years, despite her illness. His throat tightened as he met Dr. Wilkes's eyes.

"Go ahead and make the necessary preparations. I shall arrange things here so that I can retire to the country for the rest of the Season."

Dr. Wilkes pulled out a chair, sat, and cleared his throat.

"May I be frank with you, my lord?"

"Of course. You may always speak honestly," James

assured him. He had employed the doctor five years ago, and in that time, he'd grown to see the man as a friend.

"I admire the nobility of your heart, of wanting to stay with her even when her world is growing dark inside her mind." Dr. Wilkes's voice roughened, and he paused as if he needed a moment to master his emotions. "But you risk losing yourself, my lord. Your own life is frozen, but the rest of the world is moving on without you. You deserve a life too, one of joy, of marriage and children. Your mother would not want you to be without your own life for the sake of hers." Dr. Wilkes looked away as he finished, his face red with embarrassment.

For a moment, James pondered his friend's words. It was true. He wanted a life. He had let his fears for his mother trap him in a place where he'd become afraid to move forward. But he couldn't simply send her off to become someone else's concern.

Dr. Wilkes spoke up. "I daresay that the change of environment might even help her condition in some manner. I assure you I will do all that is required to keep her mind active. And when time allows, then you should join her. But not before."

"I—you may be right. I will stay in London, then, but if she needs me for *anything*, you must send for me at once."

"Of course," Dr. Wilkes vowed.

James's mind was flooded with the chaotic panic of sending his mother away mixed with the fear he'd never see Gillian again. Dr. Wilkes was right. He had to move forward, had to find happiness, and that meant finding Gillian Beaumont. He was going to start by heading to Viscount Sheridan's townhouse and seek her out there. Audrey Sheridan had to know where Gillian was.

He left the dining room and walked to his study, where he kept the most up-to-date copy of *Debrett's*. He searched page by page, looking for the name Beaumont. If she was connected to any peer, she would be here. With a little cry of triumph, he found the Beaumont name and then frowned. The Earl of Morrey was named Adam Beaumont, and he had one sister, Caroline, just as Wainthorpe had told him.

Perhaps Gillian was a distant cousin? Someone not titled and only distantly related? She would not be included in *Debrett's* if that was the case. He closed the book and slipped it back in between other gilded titles, then headed for his chambers. In a few hours, he would pay a call on Audrey Sheridan.

Or perhaps he should say, *Lady Society*.

❧

"I THINK YOU'VE GONE MAD," GILLIAN INFORMED HER mistress.

Audrey lay on her stomach on the bed, penning her next column for the *Quizzing Glass Gazette*. A sleek black cat pawed at the quill pen each time Audrey frowned and crossed a line and rewrote something in its place.

"Hmm?" Audrey murmured, clearly not listening.

Gillian rolled her eyes. She folded the red silk gown Audrey had worn the previous night, though it was perhaps beyond repair. It was tattered, and its stitching was ripped in a few places, no doubt caused when Audrey had scaled the window.

"I said I think you've gone mad, my lady."

Audrey's eyes flicked up from the paper, and she stared at Gillian.

"Mad because I'm writing an exposé on the Unholy Sinners of Hell, or mad that I brought home Archimedes?" She glanced toward the handsome black cat on the bed beside her.

"Both, I should think." Gillian stared at the black cat. The Unholy Sinners had claimed he was the devil. Gillian was not fool enough to believe such nonsense, but the cat had an eerie way of watching her. She could feel its gaze when she turned her back.

"Nonsense. We unmasked nearly all the men during the fight last night, and it's time we let the *ton* know who among them are not in fact gentlemen."

Gillian grunted in disagreement. "And what does Mittens think of Archimedes?"

"Mittens? Oh, she sulked a bit at first, but I believe she'll come around." Audrey eyed the cat critically. "He's a bit like Muff, don't you think?"

"Muff looked sweet," Gillian said, thinking of Mittens's littermate. The two ancient cats had been in the household since they were kittens. They had become a welcome presence over the years, but last fall someone had killed Muff as a message, to hurt and warn Audrey's brother. After Muff's death, Mittens had wandered around the house, crying for him to come back. She'd finally given up and settled back into her old routines, but she hadn't been the same.

"Archimedes is sweet," Audrey said.

"I highly doubt that," Gillian replied as she picked up Audrey's boots and set them in the hall. Sean would collect them soon, and they would be polished.

"Why did you name him Archimedes? I should think Lucifer would be more appropriate."

Audrey leaned over and covered the cat's ears, as though muffling anything he might hear.

"Just because he was presiding over a devil's feast doesn't mean he's a wicked cat. He might've been lured there as we were, under false pretenses."

At this Gillian couldn't help it. She laughed. "Lured under false pretenses? He's a cat. They probably snatched him from some alley in the street."

"Nonsense." Audrey sat up and cuddled the feline to her chest, nuzzling her face against his fur. "Cats never go anywhere they don't choose to. During the fight, he attacked one of the men, Lord Augersley, before I grabbed

him from the table. Yet he didn't fight me at all, did you?"
Audrey asked the cat. The cat blinked.

"Good Lord." Gillian groaned and headed for the door.
She had no desire to listen to Audrey sing the praises of a
devil cat.

Even I have limitations as to what I can endure.

"Are we really not going to talk about it?" Audrey's soft
tone stilled Gillian as she reached the door. Her hand
rested on the brass handle, and she drew in a slow breath.

She closed her eyes a moment and prayed her mistress
would not ask her about James. "About?"

"Last night. Jonathan brought me home, but you didn't
come back until early this morning. The messenger who
brought the note said you'd been injured and that James
had taken you to his townhouse."

Gillian flinched when she recalled Lord Pembroke's
note to the Sheridan house.

"Gillian," Audrey said even more gently. "I know you
have a *tendre* for him. It's not something to be ashamed
of."

"Isn't it?" The words felt acidic on her tongue as she
faced Audrey. "I'm not now and never will be suitable for
someone like him. I'm a *maid*, my lady. He is an earl. I'd be
lucky to be his mistress."

"James has never taken any mistresses. None that I
know of, anyway. And don't forget who I am." Audrey
waved her quill as she slid off her bed and shooed
Archimedes away from her letter. Gillian swore she saw

the cat reading the paper. That was how badly she knew she'd struck her head. Cats did not read.

"Gilly, we must talk about you and James."

"Having or not having mistresses is beside the point. He and I could never—" She shut her mouth, hating that her eyes were suddenly beginning to water.

Audrey walked over and gently embraced Gillian in a hug. Then Gillian burst fully into tears.

"Have a good cry. I always feel better afterward. Men simply don't understand the power of a good cry."

Gillian sniffed and let out a worried giggle. "There are far too many things men don't understand."

"That is certainly the truth." Audrey chuckled and let go of Gillian, but her face sobered again. "Let me ask you something, and I want an honest answer, even if it pains you greatly."

Gillian nodded. There wasn't much she wouldn't do for Audrey. Their loyalty to each other was almost like that of sisters.

"If you were a lady and James was an ordinary gentleman and there was no issue of risk of social standing and such nonsense, would you want to be with him?"

Gillian fought the instant denial and the need to hide her feelings and emotions. As the illegitimate daughter of a peer, she'd learned quickly that her feelings and thoughts would only lead to sorrow. But Audrey had demanded honesty, and she had promised to give it.

"Yes."

Audrey's eyes twinkled. "That's all I needed to hear." She spun, her pink gown fluttering as she sat back down on the bed and reached for her Lady Society column.

"You aren't planning on interfering?" Gillian tried to phrase the question carefully, but it still sounded accusatory.

"Interfere? Heavens no." Audrey sighed as she read over the paper. Then stopped. "I simply needed to know where you stand so that I might best deal with this matter should it come up in the future. I understand your fears. Loath though I am to say it, an earl and a lady's maid would be quite an impossible situation. But I do not wish to see hearts broken, either. So forewarned is forearmed, as they say. Rest assured, I will deal with the matter appropriately should it ever come up."

Gillian didn't trust that statement in the slightest. "Interference" might as well have been Audrey's second name rather than Helen, the one her parents had given her.

"Why do I not believe that?" Gillian muttered under her breath.

"You look a bit peaky, dear. Why don't you go down to the kitchens, have a little rest and some tea. I'll be here working on my article, and I won't need you." Audrey wasn't looking at her now, but Gillian knew her mistress's quick dismissal meant she was up to something. Gillian debated on staying to supervise her mistress, but she finally relented.

"Very well." She left the bedchamber and met Sean in the hall as he picked up the boots she'd set out to polish earlier.

"I'm fetching tea and a bit of rest. Would you mind watching over her?"

The handsome footman grinned. "Up to her old tricks, is she?"

"Afraid so. She knows I'm cross with her for running off last night to that dreadful club. She wasn't supposed to go, especially not alone."

"Aye, she's a reckless lass." Sean's Irish accent always softened his criticisms. The two liked each other very much, and Gillian knew he was worried about Audrey. Just as he worried about Gillian. Sean was the elder brother she'd never had.

"I was rather hoping she would settle down. She was so eager for Mr. St. Laurent before, but now she won't even entertain him when he comes to call."

"That's true," said Sean. "They returned here after one in the morning, looking quite tousled, both of them. Thankfully, his lordship and Lady Sheridan were both asleep. But when Mr. St. Laurent returned midday to pay a call, she refused him entirely."

That surprised Gillian. She'd come home from James's house and had been put straight to bed, where she'd rested until after lunch. She had missed the drama of Jonathan St. Laurent being turned away. And after such a daring rescue?

"I think if it was me pining after her, I would kidnap her and take her to Gretna Green. Leave nothing to chance. She needs to marry that man, but for some reason she's now set her mind against him."

Gillian sighed. "Sean, I fear you read too many Gothic novels if you believe that is the answer to my lady's problems." She was going to grow old and gray far too soon if she continued to worry about her mistress like this. But perhaps Sean had a point. If left to her own devices, she could picture Audrey coming up with no end of protests and excuses to deny him.

"Let's get you some tea." Sean escorted her down the stairs, Audrey's dainty boots tucked under one of his arms as he opened the door that led to the kitchens.

The sudden tap of the knocker on the front door made them both freeze.

"Wait here, and I'll see who it is." Sean set the boots down and headed for the door. Gillian saw the bright sunlight cut through the hall as Sean opened the door. A tall silhouetted figure stood there, his hat tucked under one arm.

"My name is James Fordyce. I'd like to pay a visit to Miss Sheridan. Is she at home?"

James! Gillian ducked halfway into the hall that went down to the kitchens and peered around the door in time to see James enter the foyer.

"I'll see if Miss Sheridan is accepting visitors," Sean said.

He hastily ascended the stairs. Gillian couldn't help but study James from her hidden vantage point, remembering him as he'd been the night before. It was as though it had been some sort of wonderful dream. The hazy darkness, the sliding of limbs, the moans and sighs, the building pleasure that had blinded her for moments before she came down from it all, shaking and weak. Had they really made love? Or had it been a feverish dream she believed to be real only because she wished it to be so?

James glanced about the hall, not seeing her in her hiding place. The tan trousers he wore clung to his athletic legs, legs that had pressed against hers in bed. His broad shoulders filled out his maroon jacket. A gold waistcoat accented the white shirt beneath, a shirt much like the one she had pulled off him last night. A flush crept over her cheeks as she tried to dispel memories from the previous evening.

Heaven help me. It hadn't been a dream, and she would never be able to pretend that it had been. It was burned into her heart.

Audrey came down the stairs a moment later and greeted James with an embrace. Gillian flinched. She knew her mistress was affectionate by nature, but she couldn't ignore the flash of green across her eyes as she watched them touch. She knew there was nothing between them, of course, but *she* was the one who wanted to be hugging James like that.

"James! Do come into the drawing room. I'll send for tea."

Gillian flattened herself against the wall close to the back stairs that led up to the servants' quarters as they passed, holding her breath as she listened to James's voice slowly fade as he moved farther and farther away.

I had one glorious, wonderful night. It's more than most women ever have. I should be thankful for what I have. A safe place to lay my head, an employer who protects me, and friends.

But after sharing a bed with the Earl of Pembroke, she knew that her life would never be the same.

5

James didn't feel like sitting, but when Audrey motioned for him to sit while she poured tea, he did the gentlemanly thing and eased into the nearest chair. He took a moment to study the lady before him. She looked bright-eyed and well, with no hint of the dark horrors she had faced the previous evening. She, like Gillian, was like no other woman he'd ever met. He was used to encountering preening, silly creatures who focused only on a man's title and wealth. These two petite Amazons with their warrior spirits surprised him...and fascinated him.

"How are you after last night? I'm afraid that due to the chaos we could not avoid getting separated. I trust Mr. St. Laurent escorted you safely home?"

"Oh yes, we were fine." She held out a cup of tea and he accepted it, taking a sip only after she sipped from her own cup. The orange pekoe was one he did not drink often, but he rather liked the subtle hints of spices upon his tongue. Audrey had excellent taste in tea.

"And Miss Beaumont? Did she return safely to you this morning?" He waited, studying her, hoping she would betray at least a hint of Gillian's whereabouts or the nature of their acquaintance. "I missed seeing her depart earlier."

Audrey's lips curved in a little smile. "Yes, she did. Thank you for taking such good care of her, James. Gillian is quite dear to me, one of my closest friends."

"Is she?" He sat forward, eager to learn more. Gillian was continually proving mysterious, raising more questions than providing answers.

"Yes, we've known each other for three years. Since we were sixteen. I trust her with all my secrets." Audrey looked him closely in the eye. "*All* of them."

He set his cup down on the lacquered table between them and glanced about to ensure they wouldn't be overheard. "She knows of your...occupation?"

Audrey nodded. "And I hope you will keep that knowledge hidden as well, my lord."

"No one shall hear it from me, but I fear your secret is no longer safe. After last night, it is quite clear that men like Gerald Langley will be out for revenge. You must take care. Both of you. Langley has seen Miss Beaumont's face, and I fear some harm could come to her." He raised his cup to his lips, planning his next words carefully. It was quite clear Audrey would protect her friend from any perceived threat, but he hoped she would see him as an ally. "Is there any way I might see her again?"

Audrey's sharp gaze settled on him again. "That depends. What are your intentions, James? As Lady Society, I don't only challenge the conventions of the *ton* with my exposé articles; I do other things as well."

James nodded. "Yes, I hear you are a matchmaker. And I'm here, begging you to help me win Gillian—Miss Beaumont, that is—over." He prayed that the edge of desperation didn't show in his voice.

She set her cup down, the clink of the china loud in the otherwise silent room. She folded her hands together in her lap, her pale green gown rustling as she shifted closer to him. The intensity of her stare was like a bright beam of afternoon sunlight, and he blinked.

"I must ask you a question. Honesty matters, so it would be wise for you to give me only the truth."

He leaned forward as well, sensing the need for secrecy in this moment.

"Of course." It never occurred to him to hide his feelings or lie, not when it came to Miss Beaumont.

"Do you love her?"

"Love?" he echoed. The word filled him with a soft warmth in his chest. But he wasn't a fool. If he said yes, Audrey would not believe him. She wanted honesty, and he would give it to her.

"I haven't known her long enough to be certain of love,

but I know that from the moment I met her something seemed to fit when I am with her. Like pieces of the puzzle sliding into place or the way the sea and the shore come together. I feel tied to her in a way that defies a more rational explanation. She is intelligent, compassionate, and brave. Everything I would want in a partner in my life."

Audrey's lips curved up ever so slightly. "And beautiful?"

"Of course. But beauty is not merely that of one's face and form. It extends far deeper, into the mind and soul. That beauty grows with time rather than fades."

Audrey settled back into her chair, a thoughtful expression on her face.

"After such a brief encounter, you can hardly know her well. What if your assumptions about her were misplaced?" Audrey's eyes were sharp.

"I'm afraid I don't understand."

"If you chose to be with her and it threatened to crumble your life down around you, what then? Would you regret it? Would you abandon her, wish you had never met her?"

James lowered his head, thinking over his response. He stared at the remnants of his tea in cup before he spoke again.

"What about Gillian's life?" he asked.

"Pardon?" Audrey didn't seem to understand him, so he continued.

"Well, you say being with her might crumble my life down around me, but would it similarly damage hers? If so, then I would have no choice but to spare us both that pain. But if you are talking about my life alone...well. I believe there are certain people in life who are worth the heartache and difficult times. For me, Gillian is that woman. I truly believe she is worth *anything*."

Audrey smiled, but there was a hint of sorrow there that worried him.

"I must warn you. Gillian's life has not been easy, and she has secrets of her own. Secrets she believes will hurt any man she loved if they were ever discovered. Are you brave enough to face her when she tells you the truth?"

James frowned. The truth? That implied Gillian was lying, or at least holding back from him.

"Is she in love with someone else? Is there another man with whom—"

"No, of course not!" Audrey assured him.

A swell of relief flooded him. "Then yes, I can brave any truth so long as I have a chance to win her."

"Good." She clapped her hands in delight and leaned forward. "Then here's what you must do. You will receive an invitation from my sister to attend a house party one week from now. You will accept. Gillian will be there. You will have your chance to win her then."

"A week." He mouthed the words, still frowning.

"You can be patient, can't you, my lord?"

"Of course." He almost confessed that he felt like he'd

77

been waiting his whole life for Gillian, but he hadn't known it was her he was waiting for until he saw her in the modiste's shop.

He could still see her face when he pulled back the curtain, thinking it was his sister who'd called for help. Instead he'd glimpsed Gillian in a lovely purple gown, her back exposed, her gray eyes wide and oh-so-lovely lips. He had wanted to hold her in his arms and kiss away all the worries that showed on her face. She seemed to be a kindred spirit. A woman who spent all of her life worrying about and caring for others like he did.

True, he belonged to the Wicked Earls' Club, but unlike the other members, he could not lose himself in gambling, wine, or women. He merely wished to vanish into the darkness of the exclusive club. It was the only way he could escape his burdens, and he despised that he needed that escape. When he was with Gillian, he felt like he could breathe again. She banished the shadows inside him. For a woman like that, he would do anything.

"We shall see you in a week." Audrey stood, and he knew she was politely dismissing him. Not that he minded. He had much to think on and still had other avenues to pursue. He wanted to see if he could meet with Lord Morrey and ask him if he knew Gillian in some way. Audrey had made it clear that the lady had secrets, yet James could not imagine anything so bad. She was too sweet to have truly damning secrets.

He retrieved his hat from a footman by the entrance.

Audrey walked him to the door, and he paused as he stepped into the sunny afternoon.

"Miss Sheridan, if you do see her, will you tell her—" He didn't want to sound foolish and sentimental. "Tell her that I'm thinking of her."

"I shall," Audrey promised.

James hastened down the steps to the street, where he summoned a coach. He rode to Jonathan St. Laurent's townhouse only a few streets away, hoping to find him home. After last night's rather desperate mission, he felt he and Jonathan were like accidental brothers in arms when it came to rescuing damsels in distress. He wished he could have asked Audrey more about why she'd been there last night and how her battle with Langley had begun and led to the events of the previous evening, but he had a feeling she would keep her secrets.

When he reached Jonathan's home, he rehearsed his appeal a dozen different ways. When he settled on one, he finally lifted the knocker and rapped on the door.

The butler who met him allowed him inside and asked him to wait while he ascertained whether Jonathan was able to receive him. He didn't take long.

"This way, my lord." The butler escorted him into a drawing room where Jonathan was standing by a window, but he wasn't alone. Godric St. Laurent, the Duke of Essex, stood beside him, and the two brothers were talking quietly. Godric had a hand on Jonathan's shoulder, giving him a brotherly pat before he turned and saw James.

"Pembroke, how the devil are you?" Godric came over and shook his hand.

"I'm well, Your Grace, and you?" James grinned at the duke.

"Good, good. Offering my brother a bit of advice on women. He's still a young pup." The duke nudged James in the arm conspiratorially. Jonathan turned to face him, and Pembroke nearly paled. The man had a black eye and wasn't smiling at all.

His night, it seemed, had been far more difficult than James's. But that was hardly surprising. Jonathan had been greatly outnumbered, taking on several men at once.

It was damned good luck he hadn't gotten more bruised.

"Not so young," Jonathan snorted, but the affection for his brother was clear in his voice.

"Yes, well, you're young enough not to just take what you want."

"And some ladies object to being carried off. Your wife certainly did." Jonathan laughed. The duke laughed as well, and the sound of the brothers was so similar that it made James smile again.

"Yes, wives object at first. But that's how you make them wives, when they're objecting."

Jonathan rolled his eyes and looked to James. "How's that for circular logic, eh?"

Godric shrugged. "It worked for me, and it will work for you. Trust me, I know that little sprite too well. She won't sit around waiting for a proposal. You can ask for forgiveness later."

Jonathan shook his head and sighed. "You don't know her like I do. I won't live long enough to reach the forgiveness stage if I cross her."

James wasn't certain which woman they were discussing, but he had a sneaking suspicion it had to be Audrey. Only a man in love with a woman would have snuck into the club last night like Jonathan had. *Like I did...*

"Well." Godric focused back on James. "I understand you two had an interesting night." Godric glanced between James and his younger brother.

"Yes, we did. A very interesting night," James replied carefully, unsure of how much Godric knew.

"As much as I'd love to stay, I best be getting back to my wife. She's most insistent we discuss nursery plans."

"You are expecting?" James grinned at the thought of one of London's most infamous rogues tending to a baby nursery.

"Yes, next winter." The duke's smile was wide, and his eyes were warm. "The baby will be born in January."

James clapped Godric on the shoulder. "My congratulations, then! Lady Essex must be thrilled."

"We both are," Godric said with a laugh. "But damned

if her delicate condition has stopped her from causing trouble. Lord, Emily has a knack for that."

Godric's words earned a laugh from Jonathan. "Emily's middle name is *Trouble*. She almost got me shot, by you, my own brother, no less."

The duke glowered in a mocking way. "Because you tried to *seduce* her. And I didn't know you were my brother, or I would have just punched you."

"Well I didn't know she was in love with you. Can't blame a man for trying when he thinks he has a chance."

Godric crossed his arms. "Yes, well she's happily married now—to me. And you have your own wife to catch."

At this Jonathan nodded soberly and muttered something that sounded suspiciously like, "Catch indeed."

"Why don't you join us for drinks at Berkley's tonight?" Godric suggested to James.

"I'd be happy to." They made their farewells to the duke and were soon left in peace. When he was gone, Jonathan exhaled, his shoulders dropping.

The air of defeat seemed unlike him. James was used to Jonathan's grins and laughter and amusing tales about his brother and his band of friends, the League of Rogues, as London had taken to calling them thanks to Audrey's depictions in her Lady Society column. But this quiet, sober man was unsettling.

"So, last night," James said at last. "How the devil did you find out about that hellfire club?"

Jonathan's lips twitched. "I could ask the same of you. I keep a close eye on Miss Sheridan. She's always in the midst of trouble."

Ah, so he had been right in assuming Jonathan had feelings for Audrey. He couldn't help but wonder what the other man thought of Audrey's secret occupation as a columnist for the *Quizzing Glass Gazette*.

"You know then that—"

"She's Lady Society? Yes, I discovered that an hour before we ended up at that infernal club. I went after her, but when I saw—" He stopped abruptly, closing off all emotion in his expression.

James pursed his lips. Jonathan was hiding something, but what? And why?

Jonathan soon recovered. "However, it seems we got out of there without much harm done. To us, at any rate."

"Indeed." James paused and then decided to come out directly and ask the question burning inside him.

"Do you know Miss Beaumont?"

"Gillian? I mean yes." He smiled. "I know Miss Beaumont."

James almost crowed with triumph. "What do you know of her? I've been trying to find out more, but no one seems to know her, and Miss Sheridan wouldn't reveal anything to me when I visited her before I came here."

Again, Jonathan's face closed down. "Oh, I mean I know her, but not in a way that would be helpful to you, I fear. How well does anyone know any person, really?"

"You were there with me in that club. She was there with Miss Sheridan. They were both in danger, and I don't know why everyone is keeping quiet about Miss Beaumont." He curled his fingers against his sides. "The woman is a bloody mystery, and it's driving me mad with worry for her."

Jonathan's expression turned from emotionless to speculative.

"You like her, do you?"

James didn't deny it. "If I could find her, I'd likely ask her to marry me, but she keeps disappearing on me at every turn."

Jonathan laughed as he walked over to a table along one wall and reached for a decanter of brandy. He poured two glasses and held one out to James.

"Well, that's something you have to get accustomed to. Women like her rarely sit still and certainly don't waste time waiting around to be rescued. The best we can do is run to keep up."

James sipped his brandy and scowled. He didn't like the thought that he couldn't seem to catch up to Gillian. That meant he might not be there to protect her when she needed him most. "Are you going to the house party at Rochester Hall next week?"

"I hadn't thought to, but my brother was just there and convinced me that I should."

"Good, we can suffer together. Miss Sheridan said I am to be invited, but it has been a while since I've attended a house party." He had turned down many offers in the last two years. His mother's illness had worsened, and he had been afraid to leave her.

Jonathan rolled his glass between his palms and faced the window again. The street front outside was filled with people and coaches.

"Do you ever feel like you're an outsider looking in on this world? Like your face is pressed to the glass? All you hear is muffled, and what you see is blurred. And most maddening of all, you can't get closer." The melancholy in Jonathan's voice burned deep into James.

"More than you know." In his own way, he did understand. Many men his age with titles like his were married or had mistresses. They were living their lives, for good or ill.

But not me. Dr. Wilkes was right. I'm not truly living.

Since his mother had fallen ill, he had become accustomed to shuttering himself from the world. It was easier not to face the things he knew he was missing. A wife, children, a life. And he felt guilty that his mother had lost hers so early in life. Gillian had changed all that.

She had awakened his sleepy heart, like a bolt of errant lightning. She'd resurrected him, reminding him of all that he could have. He knew she would never send his mother away.

"Jonathan, tell me everything about Miss Beaumont. *Please*, I need to know."

Jonathan glanced at him. "I can tell you the small

things—her favorite color, the way she takes her tea, her favorite books—but I cannot tell you much more than that. She has her reasons for her privacy."

"So I've been told," James grumbled. "Tell me everything you can."

Jonathan gave a nod of his head toward the door. "Very well, how about a game of billiards while we talk?"

James followed him. At last, he would have more pieces to the puzzle that formed Gillian Beaumont.

6

Gillian stepped down from the coach behind Audrey and faced the vast entrance of Rochester Hall. "I think this is a terrible idea."

"Nonsense. I had to watch you mope about for an entire week, and now you owe me." Audrey's smile was far too sweet, and Gillian's stomach fluttered with nerves. Her mistress was up to something again.

Gillian let the hood of her cloak fall back, even though a cold breeze played with her skirts and tugged at her hair.

"But to act like a lady when I am not one—"

"Hush. You are a lady gently born. Your circumstances after that do not make you any less a lady."

Gillian frowned. She was certain her mistress had taken leave of her senses. When Audrey told her two days before that she might need Gillian to play a larger role in her future endeavors, she had worried about what that might entail. When she was told she was to act as a lady at Audrey's sister's house party, Gillian had prayed she'd been joking. But as usual, with Audrey, she hadn't been.

"Horatia knows to put you in a room close to mine, and the servants who know you have been made aware of the situation."

"The situation?" Gillian hissed. "What exactly did you tell them?"

"That you are learning to act the part of the lady so we might be actresses in a play that some friends in London are putting on for a house party in a few weeks. They've been told you are helping me in the act and therefore must play the part of a lady in the story. Horatia knows it's really because we are perfecting our acting for espionage. She doesn't like me spying, but I convinced her that you and I would stay close to London, so she thinks it's safe enough."

"Spying? My lady—"

"*Audrey*. You'd best get in the habit of calling me that. The rest of the guests will think it too curious if you always call me *my lady*. For the next several days, you are a lady yourself. Do not forget it." Audrey dropped her own hood as they reached the entrance to Rochester Hall. It opened, and several young footmen darted past them to the coach to fetch their valises.

"You are Miss Beaumont," Audrey reminded in a whisper. "Don't forget, no matter what."

Miss Beaumont. Lord, what a mess.

"Audrey!" Horatia appeared in the doorway, one hand outstretched and the other resting on her swelling stomach. Her first child was due in a month, and she was positively glowing. The League of Rogues and their wives were well on their way to making a league of baby rogues, heaven help them all. Aside from Horatia and Emily, the Duchess of Essex, they'd only learned a week ago that Audrey and Horatia's sister-in-law, Anne, was to give birth around the same time as Emily.

"Sister!" Audrey embraced Horatia, and Gillian remained a small distance away, watching the sisters with no small amount of envy. She would never have a close, intimate familial bond like that.

"Miss Beaumont." Horatia beckoned Gillian inside and gave her a small hug and whispered, "Don't worry, everything is prepared. Simply enjoy yourself and relax."

"Thank you." Gillian forced herself to look to Horatia with her head held high. If she was to play the part of a lady, she had to make it convincing.

"You are both in the east wing, along with most of the other guests."

"How many guests are coming?" Gillian asked, then cursed inwardly. That was a servant's question, wasn't it? A lady would not care, nor would she dare inquire into the matter.

"About thirty. Mostly some local families and a few other guests." Horatia suddenly winced and put a hand to her stomach lower down.

Audrey grasped her sister's hand. "Horatia?" She and Gillian shared a concerned glance.

"It's the baby. He's kicking my... Pardon me, I must avail myself of the facilities." Horatia hastily headed down a corridor.

"Do you want us to help you?" Audrey called out.

"No. I'll be fine," Horatia assured them and quickly rushed down the nearest hall.

"The baby was kicking?" Audrey tilted her head in puzzlement. "Whatever for?"

Gillian chuckled. Her mistress knew very little about babes and birthing.

"Sometimes a babe can be positioned in a way that when they move, it can hasten the need for a lady to relieve herself."

"Oh, I see!" Audrey blushed and peered in the direction her sister had gone. "That sounds quite awful."

"It can be uncomfortable, I'm told."

Audrey turned back to her as they waited for the footmen to bring in their luggage.

"How do you know so much about babies?"

The question made Gillian smile. "My mother was open to sharing such details with me. Her mother, my grandmother, had been a midwife. We helped a neighbor deliver a baby before the doctor could arrive."

"How did I not know this?" Audrey tucked her arm in Gillian's, and they followed the footmen carrying their bags to their rooms in the east wing.

"Because I'm not sure I should be sharing this with you, what with you being so squeamish on such matters. You'd likely never want to have a child."

"I'm not squeamish!" Audrey objected.

"You are," Gillian insisted. "Remember that time you pricked your finger on your needle and the blood—"

"Oh hush! Don't remind me. It was so mortifying. It's been hard to forget how silly I felt waking up on the floor. And in front of Emily and Anne, no less." Audrey bit her lip, frowning at the memory, and Gillian gave her hand a pat.

"I wish Lady Essex and Lady Sheridan were here tonight," Gillian admitted.

"As do I. But they are leaving for Brighton with their husbands. Something to do with buying a few stud horses. Emily is most interested in joining Cedric and Anne in breeding those new Arabians."

"And Ashton and Rosalind?" Gillian asked, wondering about Audrey's other friends who couldn't make the party.

They paused at the opening of a hallway that would lead to their rooms. "In Scotland to see Rosalind's brothers and their families. They're such devils, you know, though I mean that lovingly of course. She's trying to coax them down to visit, but I suppose a castle in Scotland is far more interesting than a boring country house in southern England. Wouldn't you agree? I'd get into such delightful scrapes if I had the chance to run about a castle.

Do you think it could be haunted? Castles are always haunted, aren't they?"

Gillian laughed. "I suppose there's a ghost or two in any old house. But we really ought to get changed and see if your sister needs help with anything."

Audrey fixed her with a stern glare. "She has a fleet of servants, and you aren't one of them. Now go and change into that gown I bought you, the one with the white sash around the waist and the little white flowers on the sleeves and hem. It will be perfect for tonight. You will look fetching."

Gillian gave in to her mistress's wishes, even though she knew she had no reason to look fetching, no reason at all. The little thought made her heart ache.

They parted ways, and Gillian found her room farther down the corridor. It was strange to think she would be sleeping in this bedroom, with its stunning colors and large four-poster bed. She had gotten used to the quaint-ness of the servants' quarters, and having this much space to herself was unsettling.

She touched the blue coverlet, her fingers tracing the gold threading. She walked to the window, happy to see a view of the gardens, but her heart stopped when she saw that there were two men by a small open lawn, swinging croquet mallets as they talked.

James. James Fordyce was here, talking to Jonathan St. Laurent. For a long moment Gillian couldn't get past the shock of seeing him here. She'd believed she would never see him again, that everything that had happened between the two of them was in the past, but now...

"Oh!" She gasped as she realized Audrey would have to have known James would be coming. She always knew such details. There was no other explanation. Audrey's excuse that it was for bettering her spycraft had been a lie.

Her mistress had led her right into this. She'd betrayed her. Gillian rushed from the room and went straight to Audrey's door, pounding on it.

"Yes?" Audrey's voice came from within, and Gillian didn't wait. She burst inside and glared at Audrey.

"He's here."

"Who?" Audrey asked. Her brown eyes were wide and guileless.

"Lord Pembroke. He's here."

"James? Really?" Audrey's eyes brightened, and then her gaze narrowed. "Oh dear, you will have to see him, won't you? That does complicate matters..."

Gillian stared at her, wordless for a moment. "You...we —" She drew in a shaky breath. "You didn't invite him here for me, did you?"

"What? No, of course not. You told me you wanted to forget, to move on. We are friends, and I respect that."

"Yes," Gillian murmured. "Of course." Did she really believe Audrey hadn't meddled? She honestly wasn't sure.

"I suppose we will have to make doubly sure that he believes you are a lady, won't we?" Audrey folded her hands together, pressing her fingertips together in a contemplative fashion.

Gillian leaned back against the closed door. "Perhaps I should feign illness for the remainder of the party."

"Nonsense! We should face this head-on. You saw him? Let's go and have a little meeting and get it over with. You can say hello, he can say hello, and then we can return to the house."

"I don't think—"

"Fetch your shawl and let's go," Audrey commanded.

Gillian returned to her room and selected a white shawl that accented the dark blue carriage gown she wore. She joined Audrey in the hallway, and they walked down the hall arm in arm. Gillian had been to this house a few times in the last year, and she always lost herself in the beauty of the architecture and the marble statues in the grand hall. The Marquess of Rochester had exquisite taste.

"Where did you see him?" Audrey asked.

"In the gardens. I think they were playing croquet."

"*They?*" Audrey asked. "Someone was with James?"

"Yes. He was with Mr. St. Laurent."

Audrey jerked to a halt, her face paling. She looked like she might faint.

"You didn't know he was coming?" Gillian asked.

"No, I was told he *wasn't* coming." Audrey drew in a slow breath and raised her head. "Very well. We shall face the meeting together."

"Yes," Gillian said. "We will face them and then run back to the house with our tails tucked between our legs."

"Nonsense. We are ladies of quality, Gillian. We do not flee. We walk briskly away from that which distresses us." Audrey declared this with such a pompous, mocking dignity that Gillian couldn't help but giggle. Yet she worried about her mistress. What had happened between her and Jonathan? Was it close to what she and James...? Gillian banished the thought. Surely her mistress would not be so reckless.

They left the house and walked along the path close to a line of succession houses. There was a series of walled gardens, which were lined by wooden doors that could be locked when not in use. Gillian knew from her last visit here that the cook at Rochester Hall used the gardens to grow melons, grapes, peaches, nectarines, and even exotic blooms like orchids and carnations for decoration. The carnations were, of course, her favorite, and the last time she'd been here, Audrey's brother-in-law had allowed her to take a bloom to her quarters. She'd kept the bloom in a small cup of water for several days, watching it in the sunlight pouring through the small window of her chamber. It had been her little joy that week.

Ahead of them, Jonathan and James were putting away their croquet mallets while a footman rushed to collect the wickets on the lawn.

"James!" Audrey waved at both men near the little garden shed. Jonathan hit his head as he straightened from the shallow doorway of the little shack. He scowled and rubbed the top of his head, then turned and smiled hesitantly at Gillian as she and Audrey approached.

"Ladies!" James dusted off his palms on his trousers and grinned. "Miss Beaumont, I'm pleased to see you again, and looking so well."

"Thank you." Gillian barely stopped herself from looking down and instead met his gaze. She had to act as though they were equals. She was stunned by the dynamic vitality he exuded in that moment. He was looking at her as if they were utterly alone, back in his bedchamber where the world outside held no sway.

"Gillian, I'm going to check on the pineapples. Horatia asked me if I could."

"Pineapples?" She didn't remember Horatia asking her to do any such thing.

"Yes. The *pineapples*." Audrey gave her a knowing look and a slight nod at James.

"Oh...yes..." Gillian recovered and played along. "I do hope they are growing well."

"And that is exactly what I shall go and investigate." Audrey bid them goodbye.

Jonathan watched her go, then stomped off in the other direction with a half-muttered excuse. Gillian was alone with James again. That hadn't been part of the plan she and Audrey had agreed upon, but she couldn't find it in herself to care about the scandalous nature of the moment. Seeing him again made her forget she wanted to avoid him.

"You left before I could say goodbye," James said, drawing a step closer. His brown eyes warmed her, and for a dangerous instant she wanted to throw herself at him. Beg him to kiss her, to make her forget her worries, her dull, boring, and quiet life.

"I'm sorry. You were sleeping so peacefully, and I didn't want to wake you."

"But that's the best part of the morning, waking up beside a lovely woman. I missed it immensely." His sweet words and the tender gleam in his eyes as he drew close made her heart quiver. She couldn't believe they were here, together, talking about the night they'd shared and how he'd missed her the next morning.

He reached into his waistcoat pocket and pulled out a red carnation.

"For you. I've been told it's your favorite." He frowned as he noticed the petals were a bit crumpled. "I'm sorry, I was hoping to get it to you sooner once I learned you would be here."

She accepted the flower, her hand shaking slightly. He'd carried it around until he saw her? "How did you know it was my favorite?"

He bit his lip and grinned sheepishly. "Mr. St. Laurent relented to my begging and gave me a few details about your life, your likes and dislikes." But he hadn't told James she was a servant? She wanted to hug Jonathan, but she shouldn't have been surprised. He'd been a servant himself once and knew what hardships they faced.

James held out his hand to her in a silent invitation. *Refuse. Walk away. Be sensible.*

Gillian buried the voice beneath a surge of foolish hope in her chest. She placed her hand in his, and he led her down a garden path, away from the succession houses and walled gardens.

"So you know my likes and dislikes?"

"Yes. Let's see." He tucked her hand on his arm, bringing their bodies even closer. "You enjoy riding but don't get to do so nearly as much you would like, you adore Christmas, and you love to read more than anything else. You cannot stand the taste of duck, and you aren't terribly accomplished at drawing or playing instruments."

"Accomplished? Heavens, you gentlemen have such high standards. What I wouldn't give to be measured like a man. Am I quick-witted? Am I good with numbers in business?"

James chuckled. "I always thought a lady's accomplishments in the arts were a bit silly. I mean, it's damned impressive to see my sister's embroidery, but it gives me very little to discuss with her. Thank heavens Letty is a reader like you." He glanced her way, a mischievous grin on his lips. "If you were a gentleman, what would you do with your day?"

She pondered the question. The birds in the trees chattered lightly as the two of them crunched gravel beneath their boots, giving an eerie sense that this moment could last forever, and she wanted it to.

"I suppose I would wish to be in trade. I'm not one for sitting still. I would open a shop, a bookshop, and enjoy running it immensely."

"I like that." James chuckled. His rich and deep voice reminded her all too much of the night he had made love to her.

"And you?" Gillian asked. "If you weren't running your estate, what would you do?"

"That's simple. I'd come to work at your bookshop. I promise I could take orders quite well." He winked at her, and she flushed.

He sobered as they reached a set of stairs leading up to a terrace, as if he knew that they would part ways soon. Gillian moved up a few steps, but he turned her back to face him.

"Gillian, I want to...*know* you. I think if you gave me the chance, I could court you properly. But if you keep running away from me, I..." He grasped her hands in his. "Do you not feel what I feel?" He stared down at their hands and intertwined his fingers with hers. "When I'm with you, it's like my heart is shot through with fire and light, and yet I feel a tranquility I've never known was possible. Tell me, am I mistaken? Am I the only one who feels this between us?" When he looked up at her, their faces were on an even level because she'd taken a step ahead of him on the stairs.

"I..." A thousand yeses sat on the tip of her tongue, but she was afraid to voice them. She could not let this madness continue. "It doesn't matter what I feel. What matters is that I'm not the woman for you, Lord Pembroke. I'm sorry."

The light of hope burning in his eyes dimmed. She marveled at how even in sorrow he looked wonderfully handsome.

"Who's to say you are not? Is there another? If so, then I will..." He choked on the words. "I will relent. But if you don't..."

She should have lied, told him that she belonged to someone else, but she couldn't. "There is no other."

His eyes brightened again, and her heart jolted. "Then you feel *something* for me. If you did not, you would dismiss my wish to court you with ease."

Gillian couldn't deceive him, at least not in regards to her feelings. "I admit, it is my feelings for you that make resisting you so difficult."

Before she could react, he pulled her into his arms, kissing her. The memory of being in his embrace, skin to skin, came flooding back to her. His kisses stoked that gentle fire inside her, bringing it to a roar. In the wake of a kiss like that, she was powerless to resist.

"Please. Let me court you." His hand slid slowly down her spine, holding her to him, gentle but possessive.

"James..." She sighed his name, but no other words came out.

"Remind me how to live, Gillian. Give me a chance to show you in return. It's all I ask of you. A chance."

A chance. A chance to live. It was all she'd ever dreamed, ever hoped for, but it could never last. It could only be a beautiful illusion that would someday be exposed for the lie it was.

"Please, my love." James kissed her again, with a tenderness that brought tears to her eyes.

"I... Yes... You may court me." The moment the words left her lips, she knew she was damned, but her desire to experience life outweighed the knowledge that it would soon come crashing down around her.

He laughed in triumph as he pulled back to look at her. "Then let's go riding."

"Right now? The guests are still arriving."

"I don't give a bloody damn about them. I only want to be with you." His boyish delight and the warmth of his arms around her muddled her good sense.

"I...I suppose no one would miss us if we weren't gone for very long."

"No one shall miss us. That's the benefit of a large house party." He gripped her hand, and they dashed off toward the stables, laughing like children.

For the first time in her life, Gillian felt free.

Miss Venetia Sharpe stood on the back terrace of Rochester Hall facing the gardens, and she gasped when she saw something utterly scandalous. James Fordyce, the Earl of Pembroke, was kissing a woman. Not kissing her hand or even the somewhat risqué greeting the French did with their cheek kisses. No, this was a passionate embrace with open mouths and wandering hands.

"Good Lord!" She covered her mouth. She stared at them for a moment longer before she realized they might see her. She ducked behind the part of the house near the door that led back inside. Peering around the corner, she glimpsed Pembroke and the woman running off together, hand in hand, toward the stables. Venetia glanced about and saw a young footman just inside the door. When she approached him, he opened the door for her, and she pointed back to the gardens.

"You know that woman, the lady with the Earl of Pembroke?" Venetia, as the daughter of a wealthy viscount, knew that servants were aware of nearly everything in the house and could be counted on to gossip for the right price.

The footman glanced down at his booted feet.

"Come on, you must tell me. She is a guest here for the party. I really ought to know her name so I won't look foolish when we meet for dinner this evening."

Her words seemed to relax the young man. "That's Miss Gillian Beaumont."

"Gillian Beaumont?" Venetia tapped her chin. She

knew nearly everyone of consequence in London, and she only knew one family that bore the name of Beaumont. The Earl of Morrey and his sister, Caroline.

"Is she from London? Or does she hail from the country?" she asked the footman. Again, his gaze strayed away from her.

"I don't rightly know, miss," he said apologetically. "I'm new here, you see. Only started last week. I only know her name is Miss Beaumont because she was pointed out to me. I helped take her travel case from her coach."

"Hmm..." Venetia turned back to the window, frowning.

Lord Pembroke was considered quite a catch, and Venetia had spent three Seasons doing her best to catch his attention, but to no avail. So, naturally, to see the man she wished to marry kissing a woman in the gardens like a man would kiss his mistress was upsetting.

Venetia curled her hands into fists but maintained her composure. She knew what she must do—write to Leticia Fordyce and inform her of her brother's reckless actions. She would also write to Lord Morrey and politely inquire if he had some cousins in the country. Venetia needed to know who her competition was. She wanted to be the Countess of Pembroke, and she would do anything to secure that for her future.

7

Gillian laughed as her horse galloped ahead of James's along a field of wildflowers and wheat-colored grass. A late summer had lingered this year, leaving the field glowing with color and life. The thunder of hooves behind her made her glance over her shoulder. James was grinning astride a black gelding. Their eyes met, and he smacked his riding crop on his horse's flank. The beast took the command quite seriously, and James was suddenly racing alongside her.

"First one to the road wins!" he shouted.

Gillian leaned low over her own horse, gripping the reins tight, listening to the mare's steady but labored breaths.

"Come on, you can beat him," she whispered in the horse's ear. Then she gave her mare a kick, and the horse picked up its pace. Just enough to pull ahead.

The end of the road came all too soon. She laughed as she reined the horse until it was huffing and dancing in place.

James steered his horse close to hers, their knees touching in a light bump. "You won." She'd had the groom give her a regular saddle rather than a sidesaddle since she was more comfortable riding with her legs braced on either side. Her skirts were raised far too scandalously, but no one could see them out here.

"I believe you held him back," Gillian said, out of breath with her own excitement.

"Of course not! A man would never willingly lose."

"A gentleman might," she countered with a knowing smile. He was always the gentleman with her and would no doubt let her win.

"Perhaps. It depends on how much he likes the lady he is racing against." He guided his horse closer to hers and then glanced about. "Why don't we walk them to that copse of trees and let them graze a bit?"

"All right." Gillian started to dismount, but James was already off his saddle and gently took hold of her waist to help lower her to the ground.

They stayed close a moment, bodies pressed against each other, his breath warming her skin before he released her. James cleared his throat and stepped back, and she regained her control, brushing her dress down to loosen some dust from the ride. They walked their mounts to the trees he had pointed out and looped the reins of their horses over a low branch.

They moved through the field, side by side, neither speaking as a breeze drifted through the meadow. The white clouds above them billowed and climbed up on one another. Gillian studied the skies and looked at James. The wind teased his dark brown hair, and a faint smile played upon his lips. Never in her life had she seen anything so beautiful as the late-afternoon sun illuminating hints of red and gold amid the chocolate-colored strands of his hair.

He suddenly reached for her hand. "Tell me something about you, about your childhood." She hadn't worn gloves, and the feel of his skin against hers brought back flashes of their wonderful night together.

"My childhood?" She watched as he stroked his index finger in intricate patterns over her palm. The intensity of his focus and the sensual, tender touch filled her heart with new forbidden hungers. She'd promised that one night was all she could have with him, but fate had given her another few days. Could she take a chance and enjoy them?

"Yes. Tell me anything. I'm desperate to know you, the *real* you." His tone was beseeching, and she found she didn't want to deny him anything. She met his gaze with sudden fear. Could he know she was masquerading as a lady?

"The real me?"

"Yes. Everyone has a public face, but who we are when we are out in society isn't always who we really are." His observations of society and the people in it was a credit to the depth of his character.

"Oh." She bit her lip wondering if there might be a different James, one she'd never met. "Then I must assume the same is true of you. You should go first."

His low chuckle made her smile. "Always one step ahead of me. Very well." He eased into a relaxed sitting position on the grass, and she joined him. The gold grass of the meadow had grown to the point that when they sat it came up to their shoulders, and she felt strangely safe and hidden from the world. James still held her hand as he started to speak.

"My father loved maps. He collected them. He had maps from all over the world, and I used to go into his study when I was a boy to look at them. He had a large globe, one on a spindle that I could carefully move so it would spin in lazy circles. I loved to see the continents flying before my eyes, the gilded lettering of the country names flashing in gold light and—" He stopped abruptly, looking to the sky.

"And what?" she prodded.

"I used to close my eyes and for a brief instant pretend I could fly." He pointed to a bird circling in the distance. "Just like that, like a falcon, soaring over the world." He peeked up at her from beneath his dark gold lashes, his face slightly ruddy. "It sounds foolish, I suspect."

"No! It sounds wonderful. I have always loved to watch the hawks in the meadow, how they seem to hover on the wind as they search for mice. It's a powerful feeling, imagining the ability to fly. Even Leonardo da Vinci had such dreams. Have you seen the sketches of his flying apparatus?"

James nodded. "Indeed I have. Quite extraordinary." He raised her hand to his lips, pressing a kiss to her hand before he closed her fingers, as though sealing his kiss there.

"Your turn," he said, watching her with rapt attention.

A blush crept into her cheeks, and she felt a sudden lump in her throat. She would never get used to this man watching her in this manner, to being seen as something other than a servant.

"My father—" She cleared her throat, trying to bury the flood of emotions he brought up. "He wasn't around for much of my childhood. He had duties that kept him away. But when he was there, he used to love quizzing me. He paid for me to have excellent tutors. I wasn't sent to any finishing schools; rather, he wanted my education to be special. He often said that no child of his, regardless of gender, would be lacking in education." She paused, smiling a little at the memory.

"A man who believes in the education of women. I would have liked him."

"You would have," she agreed. "My father was kept away from my mother and I due to business so we didn't see him except for a few times a week. We used to sit for afternoon tea, and he would ask me questions. Each time I got the answer correct, he gave me a slice of pineapple. They are so rare that we didn't get to eat them very often. Yet he always tried to find one and bring it with him when he came home. I remember how he used to laugh when the cook would frown and grumble about cutting it open. It has such a thick and prickly exterior." She smiled, still able to see her father's face as he would hand her slices of pineapple.

"He sounds like a wonderful man."

"He was," she agreed. Her father had suffered so much sorrow after losing his first wife, and he had truly loved her mother and her. She only wished he had married her mother, but the match would have been beyond scandalous. Her mother had been born in a brothel and raised to please men. She'd never had a chance to live a life of quality, other than as a man's mistress. But her father had met her at a gambling hell one night and whisked her away to her own happy life—as happy as one could be, anyway. She turned her attention back to her story, trying to banish her heartache.

"He always gave himself a slice when I got a question right too." She laughed. "I wish..." Her throat tightened, and for a moment she was unable to continue.

"What do you wish?" James reached up and cupped her chin, turning her face to his. The truth of who she really was nearly slipped out, but she kept control.

"I wish I'd had more time with him before he died."

"How old were you when he passed?" James brushed the pad of his thumb over her chin. She shivered as little pulses of heat flared up inside her.

"Only fifteen. Once he was gone, I knew everything would change. I had grown up in a safe little cocoon, but when he died my mother and I struggled because he hadn't set up an allowance for us. She was always delicate, and she didn't have the constitution to survive without him. She loved him so very much." She couldn't help but think of James's mother, how alone and lost she was, how her illness had robbed her of so much of her life too soon. Despite being so different from James, she shared more with him than she'd realized.

"I was sixteen when my father died," James said quietly. "Even though my mother is still alive, I feel a bit like an orphan some days. The guilt of that tears me up at times." His voice was hoarse when he met her eyes, and then he looked away, as though afraid he'd revealed too much of his heart to her. He tilted his head back, basking in the sun. "Wouldn't it be wonderful to stay here just like this?" He leaned back on his elbows with his booted feet straight out and crossed at the ankles.

"Yes, it would," she agreed. She didn't want to think about her life without James or how it would end when the house party was over and they would both return to their lives. A sudden desperation filled her, and she leaned over, placing a hand on his chest.

"Kiss me, *please*," she whispered.

"I thought you would never ask." He reached up and curled one hand around her neck, pulling her head down to his. Their lips met with a divine fire, and she trembled at the sweetness of it. Her body came alive at his touch, demanding everything he could give to her. James seemed to sense her urgency and rolled her beneath him in the grass. He kissed her with a savage intensity, and her thighs fell apart to allow him to lie on top of her.

"I rushed last time—it went too fast. I won't make that mistake again," he vowed. "You deserve the best a man can give his woman."

His woman. Those two words turned her heart over in her chest. Despite her constantly telling him that they could not be together, everything in his actions said he would marry her tomorrow if he could. She dared not think too long about how wonderful that made her feel, because she couldn't let it happen.

She curled her arms around his neck and pulled his head down to hers. But he didn't kiss her for long. His lips moved down her throat, her collarbone, and finally to the curves of her breasts. For once she cursed the protective layer of her clothes, just as did he.

"Damned carriage dresses," he muttered.

He moved down her body, shoving her skirts up to her hips. Laughing softly, he muddled through the mountain of petticoats and undergarments until he found her hot center. He stroked her sensitive bud, teasing her relentlessly before finally slipping a finger into her, torturing her with pleasure. Gillian threw back her head, moaning at the delicious invasion. She arched her hips, urging him to push in deeper.

"You're so lovely," he breathed as he leaned over her. "So much that it hurts." The air between them sparked with invisible lightning as he leaned down and kissed her. His hand was still between her thighs, and she panted for a climax. He unfastened his trousers and moved back over her, sliding into her, filling her with his every inch. When their hips met and he was finally seated inside her, his kisses turned ravenous. His demanding mastery of her mouth made her body quake with hunger.

"James, please, stop teasing me." She clutched his shoulders, pressing beneath him, desperate to encourage him to move.

"I could stay like this forever," he murmured in her ear. "You are the one for me, love. There can never be anyone else."

His words rushed through her like a wondrous wind, sweeping her away with an explosive thrill. She felt the same, the desire to stay this way forever, to bottle it up and keep it just between them. *If only...*

The realization that this moment would end was dispelled as he began to move inside her. She ceased to be Miss Beaumont or Gillian the lady's maid and became a being of feeling and emotion, of light and heat. Rationality was obliterated as she curled her arms around him.

As their bodies joined, passion pounded deep inside her heart, moving outward until it filled her head to the breaking point. With a dull roar she shattered into a million glowing stars. Yet he didn't stop. He continued to thrust inside her as she quivered around him, the aftermath rippling through the most secret part of her. She could taste the salt on his skin, the sweetness of his mouth, and she focused on holding him within her, feeling one with him in a way she'd never dreamed. He came with a low cry and buried his face in her neck, covering her with breathless kisses. Their soft breaths mixed, and she couldn't resist savoring it, knowing it couldn't last.

"One of these days," he panted, trying to catch his breath, "I'm going to strip you bare slowly and take my time, make you come apart in my arms over and over again."

The soft glow of joy from their lovemaking was dimmed by his words.

"Is that bad? Should I not have—?" Lord, she was a wanton creature who was too base. What must he think of her, being too aroused so fast?

"No!" He laughed as he rose and settled down beside her. But when he saw her face, his laughter died and he cupped her cheek. "No, it's wonderful. You are so free with me. Do you know how rare that is?"

Gillian shook her head. "You must have been with many women."

"I haven't," James said. "Not fully. Before you, there's only been one other woman."

"What?" She sat up a little beside him. Their legs were still tangled, but she didn't try to pull away.

"I suppose it's not very roguish to admit, but I've only been with one woman before you. She was a local girl near my estate. I was a boy. My father had just died, and she comforted me. After that I just never..." He paused, seeming to struggle for words. "I'm not a saint. I've enjoyed the passions of women since then, just not fully. I never felt close enough to any of those women to want to open myself up like that again. Until you."

Gillian stared at him. She had spent the past week convincing herself that he would move on, that he could be with many other women, that what they'd shared had only been special to her.

I've been so wrong about him. So very wrong.

"Gillian?" He whispered her name, worry etching lines in his face. "What is it?"

"I..." She blushed and put a hand on his chest, toying with the buttons of his waistcoat. "I'm honored that you shared that with me."

Shadows covered his eyes. "But you still hesitate to let me court you?"

"No. I mean I do, I would like to, but it would never work between us. You must trust me when I say I cannot be the woman destined to be the Countess of Pembroke."

"Then there will never be a Countess of Pembroke while

I'm alive, not if I cannot have you. Listen to me, Gillian."
He cupped her cheeks in his hands, his eyes and voice so full
of confidence. "I am not a man who cares about his reputation. Just because I have a title and I live in London doesn't
mean I care about looking good to the *ton*, because I don't."
He stroked the pads of his thumbs over her cheeks. "I only
came here today hoping to find you. Whatever you are
worried about, I'm positive it won't matter."

But it would. He just didn't realize how much. But
Gillian knew that a servant and a peer marrying would
tarnish his reputation and destroy his sister's marriage
prospects. Any political ambition he might have would die
as well. He would be cast out, ostracized.

"If you won't give me forever, will you give me this
week at the house party?"

A week. Could she take that risk? Have seven
wonderful days to be with him the way a lady would be
with a gentleman? To live a fantasy, if only for a while,
knowing she would never have another such chance? It
was a risk, but she didn't want to refuse. What memories
they could make in a week would last her a lifetime.

She nodded. She couldn't have refused him, didn't *want*
to refuse him.

"Excellent," he said and placed a kiss on her brow.
"Let's get ourselves in order and ride back. Dinner will be
soon, and you will need time to prepare."

Gillian almost said she needed very little time, but she

couldn't forget that now as a lady there were expectations as to her hair and gown. She would have to look her best in terms of hair and clothing. She was never more thankful than in that moment for the fine gowns Audrey had insisted she bring along for herself.

"Yes, of course." She took one last look of longing out across the golden meadow and the forest beyond, then back at James. *Her* James.

One week to pretend he is mine. It will be enough.

🙚🙚🙙

DINNER WAS A DREADFULLY DULL AFFAIR FROM JAMES'S perspective. He had to spend the entire evening next to a young woman of his acquaintance, Miss Venetia Sharpe. She was a nice enough girl, but her naked ambitions always sent him running. He had no desire to marry a woman who would push him into a political career because it would further elevate her own status.

He sought out Gillian farther down the table, and their gazes briefly locked. He smiled at her as he remembered how they'd made love in the meadow. A blush reddened her cheeks, and she returned his smile, although she soon ducked her head and turned to speak with her companion.

"My lord?" Venetia leaned closer, her perfumed scent distracting. It wasn't unpleasant, by any means, but it wasn't Gillian's sweet scent of rosewater and something feminine and natural.

"Er... Yes." He reached for his wine goblet for what felt like the hundredth time that evening. Already his senses were beginning to become unsteady. He would be lucky to stand after a dinner like this.

"I recently began a correspondence with your sister, Leticia. She's a lovely woman, and when we return to London, I hope that you and she might join me for a ride in the park."

James was tempted to praise the woman for her brazen attempt to connect herself more firmly to him. If he was seen riding with Venetia and his sister, it would set tongues wagging that he would likely be marrying the girl.

"That sounds nice. I'm sure Leticia would be delighted to ride with you." He carefully chose not to confirm his own presence in that particular activity. He leaned forward and glanced down the length of the dinner table at Gillian again. At least twenty people were here at Rochester Hall for the party.

Gillian was seated between Charles Humphrey, the Earl of Lonsdale, and Jonathan St. Laurent. She seemed to be talking rather animatedly whenever Jonathan addressed her, but each time Charles spoke she blushed and glanced hastily back to her dinner plate.

A flicker of jealousy shot through him. The man was fair in looks and most amiable. He was one of James's friends, but he was also a damned rogue and a reckless seducer. James didn't want his woman anywhere near such a man. Gillian glanced around and caught his eye, offering a small smile. This time when she blushed, he knew it was because of him.

An elbow jabbed him in the ribs. Venetia stared at him in shock, looking all too innocent.

"My apologies." He realized then that the humming sound in his ears, one which had been annoying him, had been Venetia's voice.

"My lord, I really *must* tell you that your distraction is most upsetting." Her announcement drew the attention of the guests surrounding him, and his face flamed. Across the table, Lucien Russell, the Marquess of Rochester, his host, was trying to hide a snigger behind his wineglass. His wife, Horatia, was frowning at him, but then she winced and touched her belly.

James knew that many men would have shut their wives in for at least two months prior to their delivery, but Lucien hadn't. He'd confessed to James earlier that day that the thought of his wife lying on a bed for two months was unconscionable. It would drive them both mad.

"I truly am most sorry," James said to Venetia. He was relieved as the next course arrived and everyone looked toward the rich bread pudding and a tower of red and blue jellies that were carried in. Several people applauded at the sight, and James took the opportunity to steal another glance toward Gillian.

Ten people separated them, and he could barely stand

it. If he had to survive an entire week without sitting beside her at a meal... Perhaps he could convince Horatia to change the seating arrangements each evening. It might give him a chance to sit closer to Gillian at least once without offering offense to Miss Sharpe. She'd clearly set her cap for him and wouldn't be deterred.

As dinner came to an end, James was ready to flee to the billiard room along with the rest of the gentlemen. He would find a way to get to Gillian tonight, once the lamps were doused and most of the servants had gone to bed.

He paused in the hallway as the ladies withdrew from the dining room and proceeded toward the drawing room. Gillian looked his way. He smiled again, trying to ignore that boyish rush of hope each time she smiled back.

"You'd best watch yourself, Pembroke," Lucien said as he joined James in the hall.

James glanced toward Lucien. "I beg your pardon?" The redheaded devil was grinning.

"I see you've got your eye on one lady, but another is out to leg-shackle you."

James sighed and then laughed. "The claws of Miss Sharpe are long indeed. I thought I wouldn't survive past the third course."

Lucien patted him on the shoulder. "Come and play a game. You can forget all about scheming ladies."

The billiard room was full of gentlemen pouring glasses of port, and at least four men were ringed around a lacquered box, plucking cigars out. Charles lifted one to his nose and sniffed, then grinned and tossed it at James. James caught it as he and Lucien joined Charles.

"Long night ahead, I should think," Charles said.

"How so?" James asked.

"The ladies will be up late. They were all a little too lively. It means we will be up late to keep a watchful eye on them." Charles's tone held a hint of mischief.

"True." Lucien's eyes strayed to the door. James realized he had to be thinking of his wife and her condition.

"Lady Rochester still has a month before the birth, doesn't she?" James wasn't sure how delicate he ought to be when speaking of her condition.

"Before the birth, yes, but..." The man's eyes were shadowed with worry. "She's been having pains today, and I don't like to be too far from her."

"Hence our role as night watchmen." Charles chuckled. "Jonathan, bring that port over here."

Jonathan retrieved a set of glasses as well as the bottle and carried them over on a tray. He set them down on the table near the billiards.

Lucien reached for an empty glass and poured himself a healthy amount of port. "Excellent—"

The door to the billiard room burst open, and Gillian rushed in, breathing hard. Her cheeks were flushed, and her bosom heaved against her tight bodice. James frowned. Something was wrong. Gillian wasn't the sort of woman to storm into a billiard room.

"My lord!" she called out to Lucien. "Lady Rochester,

her water has broken." She stared at Lucien as every man in the room leapt to their feet.

"Horatia?" The glass slipped from Lucien's hand and shattered at his feet.

"The baby, it's coming early. You must fetch the doctor at once."

"Early?" The word was a harsh whisper. Even men knew a little about babies and that a babe born too early would have to fight to survive.

"Yes." Gillian turned to James then, her gaze beseeching him to help. Lucien was too shocked to react.

"What can we do?" James asked, his heart racing.

"The doctor. We need the doctor," Gillian repeated.

"I'll fetch him," Jonathan volunteered.

"Yes, go now, Jon," said Charles. "Hurry." Jonathan sprinted from the room. Charles looked to James and nodded in Lucien's direction in a silent command, which James immediately understood. Both he and James grabbed Lucien by the arms and jolted him into moving.

"Come on, old boy, let's go upstairs and see what we can do," Charles murmured soothingly to Lucien. The once notorious rogue, who'd faced a duel against his own best friend, was now pale-faced and shaken. The rest of the men returned to their drinks and cigars, knowing it was best to stay out of the way unless called upon.

James, Charles, and Lucien followed Gillian up the stairs to a bedchamber.

"She's in bed resting, my lord," Gillian said. "But she's asked for you to come inside."

James was a little surprised. Men usually stayed out of the way, or at least he'd been told that was the proper thing to do. But if Lucien felt about Horatia the way James did about Gillian, he wouldn't want any woman he loved facing this moment alone.

Lucien was shaking as he turned to his friend. "Charles, you helped when your little sister Ella was born, didn't you?"

"I did." Charles's normally jovial manner had vanished. "It was a birth late in my mother's childbearing years, and we feared neither she nor Ella would survive. I was lucky enough to witness what was done, and I learned from one of the maids how to help."

"Until the doctor is here, could you help us? We have no one trained in birthing here. My mother is visiting my brother Lawrence and his wife, Zehra, in London. I don't want Horatia to face this alone if you know what to do."

"Of course." Charles and Lucien entered the bedchamber and closed the door.

Gillian turned to James.

"What can I do?" he asked her. "There must be something."

She nodded. "Get the footmen to bring boiling-hot water and as many clean cloths as they can. And a blade, one that's been cleaned by the fire's edge. We'll need that if the babe comes soon."

He swallowed hard. "A knife?"

"Yes. There is a cord that must be cut when the babe arrives."

"Right...Well, I'll get the knife and the rest." He grabbed her by the hips and pressed a hard, desperate kiss to her lips before he ran to find the servants.

8

G illian touched her lips, lost in the sudden rush of emotions she felt in James's kiss. Then a cry from the room behind her had her rushing back inside. Horatia was crouched beside the bed, and groaning in just a nightgown.

Lucien gripped one of her hands, his other arm at her lower back. She panted and puffed out several quick breaths and then relaxed. Audrey hovered nearby, her hands wringing fretfully.

"Does it hurt much?" Audrey asked her older sister.

"*Ah!*" Horatia clenched down on Lucien's hand.

He winced. "God's teeth! Where does a woman find such strength?"

"I think it's safe to say it hurts a great deal," Charles said to Audrey. "Why don't you see if we can't get some chips of ice or cold cloths soaked in water?"

"Right." Audrey turned to Gillian. "Did you hear that?"

"Yes, my lady, I can fetch them," Gillian reassured her.

"Thank you." Audrey hugged her and then turned back to her sister.

"I think I need to lie down...catch my breath," Horatia gasped. Lucien helped her onto the bed. She lay on her side for a moment before she groaned and then rolled onto her back, legs up. Gillian rushed to cover her parted legs with a blanket.

"Lucien, did you have a birthing chair prepared?" Charles asked.

"No, we weren't ready." Lucien's face was pale as marble.

"That's alright." Charles looked to Horatia. "You can lie on your side for the birth if you want to. If you feel the need to push, push," Charles said. "If you need to get up again and move about, we'll assist you," he instructed. There was a tenderness there that Gillian had never seen in the Earl of Lonsdale before. He was usually focused on seducing women and getting into trouble, though not necessarily in that order, but right now he was solely focused on helping Horatia deliver a healthy child.

Lucian took a seat beside Horatia. He held one of her hands and stroked her hair back from her face, murmuring softly to her. Charles moved next to Horatia on her other side, holding her free hand and checking his pocket watch. Gillian stepped outside and found a couple of upstairs maids waiting.

"We need some ice from the icehouse, broken into chips, and some cold water and cloths."

"Yes, miss." The maids dipped in curtsies and rushed away. When Gillian came back in, Audrey and Charles looked her way.

"James and some maids are having what we need brought up."

Charles sighed wearily. "Good. Because the babe is coming fast. The doctor may not arrive in time, and we shall need to be ready to deliver the child without him."

"All of us?" Audrey said, wide-eyed. Fearless as she was, Gillian's mistress was a bit faint-headed around blood. This would not be easy for her.

"Audrey, you *must* stay," Horatia pleaded. Her body was then seized by a particularly painful contraction.

"Of course I will," Audrey promised, though her face was pale and ashen.

Charles pocketed his watch and looked to the others.

"There's very little time between her pains," Charles said, and then he touched Horatia's face and forehead. "Horatia, have you been feeling pains all day?"

She bit her lip and nodded. "Yes, I just thought the babe was restless and kicking. I didn't know it was coming, not until just after dinner."

"That's all right. Babies sometimes come without warning. How are you feeling?"

Horatia gasped. "Like I need to push..." She ended in a groan, her body bowing forward. Then she relaxed and faced Lucien, panting. "The nursery, you finished the cradle? Do they have the clothes ready?"

"Yes," Lucien promised, pressing kisses to her hand. "I should've known you were ready to have our child so soon. How did I not see it?" He bowed his head, his ruddy hair glinting in the firelight. Gillian ached for him in that moment, knowing how afraid he was for his wife and child.

"Know? How could he know?" Audrey asked Gillian.

"Some women intuitively know the baby's coming and try to get everything ready. It's a bit like birds when they start constructing their nests in spring."

"Oh." Audrey stared at her sister, her brows drawn together. Gillian touched Audrey's arm.

"It will be all right," Gillian said, praying it would be. An early birth could be difficult and dangerous for both the mother and the child.

"Horatia, if you feel the need to push, then push. Gillian, I need you here," Charles said.

Gillian came over to the bed, and Charles pointed to Horatia's legs.

"Pull down the blanket and watch her for me. Keep her legs open, and I'll tell you what to look for. Normally a woman would deliver on her side, but I think Horatia is more comfortable on her back."

"Yes, my lord." Gillian knelt in front of Horatia's legs and peeled the blankets away.

"I'm frightened," Horatia said suddenly, her knees

starting to close, but Gillian grabbed her knees and kept them open. Then Gillian looked to Lucien.

"Distract her, my lord. That might help."

"Distract...?" Lucien's voice drifted a moment, and then he stroked Horatia's face. "Remember that night at the midnight garden when we talked about the stars?"

Horatia laughed, though the sound was tense. "Yes. I remember I felt so safe with you."

Lucien chuckled. "You were safe, very safe. You know I'd do anything to protect you."

Another labor pain came, and Horatia hissed and turned a vengeful eye on Lucien. "You did this to me! Oh!" She clutched at her stomach, and then a few moments later she relaxed a little.

Horatia glanced at her husband. "I'm sorry, I didn't mean to...I know you only want to help. I would do the same for you."

"I know, love, I know. And you're very safe right now. Charles knows what to do, and so does Gillian."

"Tell me a story," she begged Lucien. "A good one."

He beamed a smile at Horatia. "Did I ever tell you about the time when Cedric and I were caught sneaking back into our residences at Cambridge one night? We could barely walk from the night's revelries, and we were dragging a statue of Sir Isaac Newton, which we'd stolen from another college..."

And just like that, the room relaxed as Lucien told her about his antics during university and Horatia calmed.

Each time she had a labor pain, everyone in the room held their breath until it passed.

Gillian relaxed as Lucien kept his wife's attention. Charles coached Gillian to watch for the child's head. When a patch of dark color emerged, Gillian wanted to weep with relief.

"I see it. The babe!"

Charles crouched over the bed beside Horatia, gripping her other hand. "Good." Gillian knew he must have been in pain because Horatia's fingers were leaving angry red marks on his skin as she squeezed, but he didn't complain.

"Lucien, hold her hand, don't let go."

"I won't," Lucien answered, never taking his eyes off his wife.

Charles used his other hand to brush his knuckles over Horatia's forehead. "Now, Horatia, push when you can, and push *hard*. Time matters now. You've been in labor too long and we don't want the child to become stuck and it may suffocate."

"Suffocate?" Horatia and Lucian both hissed in alarm.

"Yes, so you'd better bloody well push!" Charles said firmly.

Horatia screwed up her face in a snarl with a guttural cry and pushed.

JAMES AND A FOOTMAN RUSHED UP THE STAIRS, A HEATED knife, water, and towels in their arms. Horatia's next scream rent the air, and James nearly stumbled but caught himself as he reached the top stair. When he reached Lucien's room, he almost rushed in, thought better of himself, and knocked. Audrey opened the door, her face white as she grabbed the items from the footman. When she saw the knife, she just jerked her head for James to enter.

"I don't think I should—"

"My sister does not care," Audrey cut in. James followed her inside, eyes downcast until he spotted Gillian at Horatia's feet.

Bloody hell...

Charles rushed over to James and grabbed the knife. "Be ready to catch the babe, Gillian."

James pressed himself against the wall, feeling useless and in the way, but he couldn't make himself leave. He was fixed on Gillian as she reached beneath the tent of Horatia's nightgown-clad legs and suddenly pulled out a small blueish-skinned baby. It was sticky and a little bloody and unmoving. He didn't know much about children, but shouldn't it have been crying?

"I need a towel," Gillian said, looking around.

James was finally able to move and rushed over to her at the same moment Charles did with the knife. James had a moment of childish squeamishness and closed his eyes while Charles cut the cord and Gillian wrapped the baby up with the towels, gently removing the blood from its tiny features.

"Is it all right?" Horatia's weak voice came from the bed. "It's not crying..."

Gillian held the baby out to the others, uncertain of what to do. James saw at once by the baby's blue face and hearing the soft little hissing sounds it made that it was struggling to breathe. Charles took the bundle from Gillian's arms and held the child close, whispering to it and pressing on its chest. James joined him, leaning over to watch the child, praying under his breath.

"Come on, little one. Breathe. *Fight.*" James willed every bit of his own strength into the child. Its face was so small, tiny hands clenching and unclenching as his little lungs struggled to breathe. Everyone in the room was silent except for Horatia, who suddenly started to cry. Lucien's gaze was torn between his wife and the child Charles held.

"Come on," Charles growled, peering down at the child. "Come on, *breathe.*"

"Please, little one, fight!" James breathed with all his heart.

The little babe suddenly pinched its face and let out a deafening wail. James relaxed; the sound of a baby's fitful scream was the most welcome thing he'd heard all day.

"If he's able to scream like that, I'd say he's got a fighting chance," Charles said with relief. He walked over to the bedpost and sagged against it, still cradling the child. Horatia and Lucien were wide-eyed and anxious as Charles handed the baby down to them.

"He?" Lucien asked.

"The child's a boy. You're a father." Charles grinned. "And I just won ten pounds off Jonathan."

"Damnation, that means I owe Godric at least thirty," said Lucien. "I was certain it was a girl. Only girls cause this much trouble."

Horatia let her head fall back on the pillows, groaning. "You stupid men were betting on my child? Do you think this was for *fun*?"

Charles and Lucien looked at the ground.

"Well, it had been rather fun, right up until this moment," Lucien admitted.

Horatia hissed. "Wait until I get my strength back. You deserve a good kick in the arse!"

"Language, my love, language. Can't be offending our new babe's delicate hearing."

Charles snorted. "Lord, he doesn't stand a chance with the League as his uncles." The earl puffed his chest out with pride. "Just wait until the others see him! What a strong lad he'll be!"

James couldn't resist grinning as he listened to their banter. He walked closer to Lucien.

Lucien stared down in wonder at the child. "He'll be the strongest of them all. Won't you, my dear boy?" Then he kissed the infant's head before placing him in Horatia's arms. She sat back against the bed. A smile hung on her lips despite her obvious exhaustion and frustrations.

"Thank you, thank you all," she said to the occupants of the room. "You saved him—you saved us both. I don't know what would have happened if..."

James only nodded. There was a lump in his throat. He looked at Lucien and Horatia as they held their son, and then he saw Gillian watching them, one hand covering her mouth. When she looked away, their eyes met and held.

"Would you wait for me outside? I must see to her ladyship, there's still a bit of afterbirth for her to deliver and then I'll be right out."

"Of course," he promised and stepped outside. Something niggled at the back of his mind, however. Something she'd said.

After half an hour, the door opened and Gillian emerged. When she saw him, her face lit up with a tired smile.

"The mother and child are still well?" he asked.

She nodded. "Once the doctor arrives, we will be sure. An early babe like him will face a difficult few weeks, but if she keeps him warm and keeps his cradle in the sun, I think he will be all right. My mother said that sunshine can cure many ailments in children."

"Thank the Lord." James opened his arms, and Gillian walked into them, burying her face against his chest. Her body trembled against his, and he realized that she must be very close to Horatia to worry so much about her. James pressed his chin on the top of her head.

He wasn't sure how long he held her, but eventually he heard her say, "Take me to bed?"

James smiled to himself. "It would be my greatest pleasure."

He took her by the hand, and they slipped down the stairs toward his bedchamber in the west wing. He planned to make love to her tonight and to finally take his time doing so.

GILLIAN TRIED NOT TO TREMBLE AS JAMES CLOSED THE door and slid the latch into place. When he turned to face her, he was smiling.

"I'm not rushing this time." His voice was soft and teasing.

"I don't want you to." She offered her back to him, and he came up behind her, his hands settling on her hips before they slowly slid up to her laced back. He threaded his fingers through laces of the gown. His gentle touch teased her.

"Maybe you want to move a *bit* more quickly?" she suggested, her voice breathless.

James's low chuckle made her skin tingle in anticipation. He leaned down and feathered a kiss on her bare shoulder.

"A little faster, then." He nibbled her neck while his fingers plucked at the dress. It soon fell into a puddle at her feet. She slipped out of her petticoats and then worked at her stays. She couldn't resist leaning backward to rub her bottom against him as she let her stays fall away.

"Lord, how you tempt me," he growled.

Gillian shivered with desire at the rumbling sound. He was always so controlled, so gentlemanly, but when he was with her, like this, he always seemed on the verge of losing that control, and she liked it. It meant he wasn't hiding anything from her—he was being himself. He was like this because of her.

She turned to face him, wearing only her chemise, and reached for his cravat. He caught her hands and pressed kisses into her palms.

"If I let you strip me bare, I won't be able to stop myself, and I want you sated and exhausted long before I have my own way with you." His smile turned positively devilish, and Gillian couldn't stop the flood of wet heat between her thighs in response.

"Is that so?" She tilted her head, offering him her neck. He licked his lips and grasped her by the waist, setting her down on the bed. She fell back, loving the way he pounced on her. James caged her with his body as he nuzzled her neck. Then he sat back, straddling her as he lifted her chemise up and off her body.

Being trapped beneath him, completely naked, made

her feel so very vulnerable, but not afraid. Being with him had never filled her with fear.

James cupped one of her breasts, his hand caressing the sensitive peak. Gillian arched her back, pressing her breast more thoroughly into his palm. He gave a low groan. His hips rocked against her, and she could feel the hard press of his arousal between her thighs.

"James, I don't want to go slow." Gillian clutched his arms, tugging on the fine white fabric of his shirt.

"What do you want?" he asked, cupping her other breast now, massaging it before he leaned down and took the nipple into his mouth. The feel of his mouth on her skin made her whimper. Sharp hunger stung between her thighs, the pain of her need rising to a fever pitch.

"I need you! Don't be gentle, not this time," Gillian begged. James tore at his waistcoat and shirt and pulled his trousers down just enough to free himself. Gillian reached down, taking his shaft and guiding him into her.

The thrust went deep, so deep she swore she could feel him everywhere inside of her all at once, as though there was no part of her that was not connected to him.

"Look at me," he said. "I want to see your eyes." James withdrew and thrust again and again. Gillian released a shaky breath as she held his gaze.

They made love frantically, as though the world might soon end around them. Waves of ecstasy built into a tempo that matched their rapidly beating hearts. It was like nothing Gillian had ever experienced, this desperate union of bodies. The feel of his eyes on her, devouring the sight of her as he possessed her in a way that made her feel wild and yet safe.

The turbulence of her emotions tonight, watching James talk to that woman during dinner, and then seeing Horatia and her child in danger and James holding the baby, willing it to live... She'd been driven to a state of desperation, a need to be with him in a way she would never regret, even if it could never last. Any reservations she had about denying herself a few more days with him were over.

"Ah!" She gasped in sweet agony as a climax roared through her. Seconds later James whispered her name, a look of wonder and shock on his face as he let go.

He lowered his head until his forehead touched hers, and he closed his eyes, breathing hard.

Gillian held him, her arms curled around his body. He was such a good man, a wonderful man, a man she was falling hopelessly in love with.

"Are you all right?" he asked, his voice low and rough. "I didn't hurt you?"

"No," she assured him. "That was remarkable." She stroked the tips of her fingers along the back of his neck, playing with his dark hair.

"That feels nice." He shifted around so that they rolled onto their sides. He kicked his trousers down off his body and shed his remaining clothing before he helped pull the coverlet back and they both climbed in.

"I keep trying to seduce you slowly," he said, smiling at her.

"Perhaps I don't need slow?"

"Hmm." He pursed his lips in a mock frown, and she giggled. "Shall I put out the candles?"

"Not yet. I want to lie here in your arms and look at you." Gillian snuggled up to his lean, muscled body, clutching him as though he were precious.

"I won't argue with that." He wrapped an arm around her and folded the other behind his head. They lay there for a few silent moments before she spoke.

"I was so afraid tonight for Horatia and her child." She held her breath, afraid to confess something like this. What if he didn't wish to talk about it?

"As was I. I've never been around a birth before. It was quite terrifying."

"I've been around one once. A neighbor who lived next to my mother and me went into labor, and we assisted before the doctor arrived."

"You don't talk about her very much," James said.

"Who?" Gillian lifted her head to look at him and rested her chin on his chest.

"Your mother. Would you tell me about her?"

Gillian was silent a long moment and pressed a kiss to his chest before she spoke.

"I loved her very much, but she wasn't strong. She chose to be with my father because she thought it would give her a certain advantage, which it did, for a time, but after his death, she didn't know what the cost would be to live alone."

"Your father left no provisions for you?"

"I'm sure he had plans to at some point, but he never told us of anything before he died." It wasn't quite the truth. Her father had given her some small funds before he died, but he could not have left the estate or even a simple portion of it to them, not without the new heir, her half brother, having the power to rescind their father's largesse. Gillian swallowed thickly and continued.

"I was sensible, had always been sensible, and I found a way to survive, but his death took a toll on my mother, and she died from the strain. Sometimes..." Tears burned her eyes, and she stopped. James threaded his fingers through her hair. The touch was soothing, and she willed herself to continue.

"Sometimes I feel relieved that I carry no more burdens, that I must rely only on myself. But at the same time, I hate feeling that relief."

He cupped her cheek, and his smile changed to one of sorrow. "I know how you feel. I love my mother, but sometimes I feel the most awful weight of her care crushing me. And I think about how the woman she was, the woman I loved, is gone and there's barely a shell left and I miss her. It makes me feel so bloody empty inside."

He paused, his voice catching. "Dr. Wilkes convinced me last week to send her to my estate in the country. He's worried about her falling. I didn't wish to, but she needs a safer place, one with fewer staircases. There's a tightness in my chest when I think of it all. Makes it hard to breathe. The only time I ever forget my worries is when I'm with you. It's like I can breathe again." James's earnestness tore at Gillian's heart. She felt the same way about him.

She moved up his body until they were nose to nose, and she kissed him, letting all of her sorrow, her joy, her *everything* flow from her lips to his. How could she deny this man anything? He was her world. For now.

But perhaps for now was all she needed.

9

etty Fordyce waited nervously in the entryway to the Earl of Morrey's townhouse. A letter was inside her reticule, a letter full of salacious gossip, but Letty needed answers, and this was perhaps the one place she could get it.

The butler appeared. "My apologies for the wait. His lordship will see you now."

Letty followed the servant to a room on the second floor. She entered the drawing room and was struck by the general attractiveness of the furnishings. The Earl of Morrey had fine taste. A figure rose from a chair as she came deeper into the room. The man was tall with dark hair and striking gray eyes that made her knees oddly weak as he smiled at her. His face was attractive too, quite so, but it was his eyes that held her attention. They so reminded her of someone, but she couldn't quite place who it was.

"Lady Letticia?" His voice was low and gentle, and the cadence of his speech held a hint of familiarity and inti-macy that made her shiver. He spoke like a lover—not that she knew what a lover was supposed to sound like, but the ones in her fantasies sounded like this, *smiled* like this.

Oh dear...

"My lord, I'm terribly sorry to disturb you, as we've had no real acquaintance until this moment." She tried to still the sudden flutter in her chest. When had a man ever made her feel so odd? Perhaps it was because it was her first time with the man and the awkwardness behind her errand—that must be it.

"It's quite all right. Please sit. Tell me why you've come. I admit your letter this morning was most intrigu-ing. What it lacked in details it made up for with a sense of mystery."

She slid onto the couch, and he resumed his place in the chair facing her.

"This will be quite an unpleasant question—at least I fear it might be. Do you know a woman by the name of Gillian Beaumont?"

Morrey's keen gaze suddenly softened. "Gillian?" He spoke the name softly, as if he'd been visited by a ghost of the past.

"Yes. You see, my brother, the Earl of Pembroke, has

recently formed a *tendre* for this woman. She said her name is Gillian Beaumont. I've never met her before, and she's not one of the *haute ton*. You are the only Beaumont I know of. I thought perhaps she is a distant cousin or a relative from the country. I only wish to know more about her, in case my brother's affections for her grow."

Morrey was silent a moment.

"I know only one woman named Gillian Beaumont."

"And she is a relative?" Letty asked hopefully. She liked Gillian quite a bit, but a letter that had arrived that afternoon, addressed from an acquaintance, Venetia Sharpe, had raised some concerns. Venetia had implied that James and Gillian had been seen in an inappropriate amorous embrace in a very public setting.

"No, not a cousin. She is, I believe, my late father's illegitimate child."

"What?" Letty stared at Morrey, stunned by his frank answer.

"I'm sorry, my lady. I should have answered with more tact. Hearing her name has left me shocked. You see"—he paused, his eyes serious—"I've been looking for her for several years now."

Letty's grip tightened on her reticule. "You've been *looking* for her?" She didn't understand.

Morrey stood and walked over to the fireplace, bracing one hand on the mantle. "Despite the fact that our acquaintance is mere minutes old, I will confide in you, Lady Letticia, because I should like to enlist your aid." He

glanced at her, a rueful smile hovering about his lips. "My
mother died when I was young and my sister was a mere
child. My father's loneliness was immense, and he sought
comfort with a mistress, a woman named Elizabeth
Brookstone. She was not of the peerage, but rather the
daughter of a gentleman who'd fallen on hard times. As my
father lay dying, he confessed the affair and the existence
of a child, Gillian. He told me he had intended to leave
them an unentailed property that had tenants, and it
would have provided them with a small income, but he
was too ill to summon his solicitor to make those changes.
I tried to get a man to our house in time, but he didn't
arrive until an hour after my father passed away. While my
father lay dying, he asked me to look after them. But in
my grief following his death..." Morrey paused. "I failed.
By the time I was ready to find them, my half sister and
her mother were gone, and I had no information to find
them. Word came to me that my father's mistress had died
and my sister had entered service, but I could not find her.
I assumed all those years ago that she was going by the
name of Brookstone like her mother, but now I know that
she must have taken the name of Beaumont. It's possibly
my father insisted on that when she was born. I honestly
don't know."

"She went into service?" Letty asked.

"Yes. As a lady's maid."

Her brother was infatuated with a servant? It took a
moment for Letty to comprehend this. But the more she

thought about it, the more it made sense. Gillian had been nervous, tentative, hesitant, yet Letty and James had forced their initial interactions upon her.

She tried to avoid us. She knew it was not proper, but we pleaded with her to come with us to Gunter's and the bookshop. Letty could not fault Gillian for that deception, but how had she and James renewed their acquaintance at the Rochesters' house party? Surely Gillian was not still masquerading as a lady?

"You say you know where she is now?" Morrey left his vigil at the fireplace and came over to her.

She had to lean back to look up at him. *Lord, he's tall.* "I believe so, yes. She is at the country estate of the Marquess of Rochester."

"But you do not know where she will be after that?"

Letty shook her head.

Morrey sighed. "I know Rochester, but not well enough to show up at his house unannounced. Certainly not during a party."

"If my brother is"—Letty paused—"attached to her in some way, I'm sure he will know how to reach her. I could inquire for you."

Morrey clasped her hands in his, and she reveled in the heat of that touch. There was something about Morrey that enchanted her. It wasn't simply the elegant line of his jaw or the luminous silver of his eyes. There was a hint of warmth in his face that suggested if he were to smile she would be utterly lost in his expression.

"Please write to me once you know. I long to meet her, to fulfill my promise to my father."

Letty stared at their joined hands before he slowly released her.

"It doesn't bother you that she was born under such circumstances? That she has spent several years in service? Most men would wish to have nothing to do with her, imagining it looked poorly upon their family." Letty hoped he was a man of his word and truly wished to help Gillian.

Morrey's lips thinned. "I cannot judge the girl for having been born. My father clearly cared about both the mother and the child. I am human enough to understand temptation and its consequences. If it had been me, I would want someone to care for the woman I loved as well as any children, no matter the circumstances of their birth." He smiled slightly. "If I have a second sister out there, I wish to know her."

Letty's throat tightened. "That's incredibly noble of you."

He chuckled. "Noble? I would rather hope it makes me human. Lord knows I'm nowhere near as noble as I wish to be."

"I will write as soon as I have news," she promised.

Morrey escorted her to the front door of his home but caught her hand before she could leave.

"Is your brother in love with my half sister?" he asked.

"I believe so."

"And she loves him?"

THE EARL OF PEMBROKE

Letty shrugged. "I could not say. She swore at our first meeting that she had no designs upon him. So for them to be together at the house party is puzzling."

Morrey seemed to sense her thoughts. "You do not approve of the match?"

"It's not that I *disapprove*, but he does not know her—he doesn't know her past or her circumstances. A relationship needs truth to survive. And I fear the situation would harm James's standing. We are of a noble house, and we can weather some scandal, but I'm not sure we could weather him marrying a lady's maid. In fact, what I question most is her motives if she continues a charade like this, if that is indeed what is happening. Once I know more, I can form a better opinion. I would hate to rush to judgment, but my brother James is too kindhearted. I won't let a fortune-hunting servant take advantage of that kindness if she has no real feelings for him."

"I understand." Morrey studied the street behind her for a moment before he looked back to her. "I hope something might work out if they do indeed love each other."

"As do I, Lord Morrey, as do I."

Letty did not wish to deprive anyone of love, but a scandal could destroy more than just James and Gillian's reputations. It could destroy Letty's future as well.

Three glorious days had passed at the house party, and Gillian had never been happier. She ignored the whispers in the back of her mind that it would all have to end and instead focused on the present. She and James were seated in the library, reading side by side, her right hand entwined with his. The rest of the guests were spread across the house and grounds, spending their free time as they wished. Gillian had tried to tempt James back to bed, but he merely laughed and told her that even the worst rogues didn't do such things until after nightfall. She sensed he was teasing her, but she was uncertain how to tease him back. She wished she could be as carefree as he was, to see the world with such promise. But the reality of her circumstances would catch up with her all too soon.

James leaned over and kissed her cheek, and the soft pressure of his mouth on her made her shiver. She leaned closer to him.

"Perhaps we might make use of my bed after all." He chuckled, but then he froze, looking toward the window behind them.

"What is it?" She started to turn, but James was already getting to his feet.

"A rider just came to the house. A rider wearing the livery of *my* family."

She followed him as he strode to the library doors and hurried into the corridor.

Why would a rider come here from Pembroke? It was a two-hour journey by horse, according to James.

Gillian stilled as James reached the entrance hall ahead of her, just as a Rochester footman opened the front door. She could think of only one reason why a rider would come here. A very terrible reason. Gillian rushed down the corridor to reach James as he was handed a letter by the messenger. James tore open the wax seal and unfolded the parchment, his eyes scanning the hastily scrawled lines before he suddenly staggered, catching himself against the wall by bracing against it with one hand.

"James, what's happened?" She reached him, clutching his other arm to support him. He swallowed hard and blinked, his eyes overly bright.

"My mother...she's dying. I must leave at once."

Gillian could feel his pain as though it were her own. "Dying?"

"She has pneumonia. Dr. Wilkes said she is fading fast. There isn't much time." His hands shook as he pocketed the letter.

There was no way he could ride in this condition alone, but he wouldn't stay here, either.

"I will go with you. I could have a coach called around," she suggested.

James shook his head. "There isn't time for a coach. I must ride—it's far quicker. And you mustn't leave. It wouldn't be proper for—"

"Hang propriety. Why must things always be so complicated with the nobility? She's your mother and you love her, and I love you, so I must go with you."

LAUREN SMITH

She almost clasped her mouth. Had she said that aloud? He turned to her, stunned for a moment, and grabbed her by the shoulders. "You love me?"

There was no point in denying it. "I do, but now isn't the time for such declarations. We must leave immediately."

The pain in his gaze cut her, but she didn't waver. When you loved someone, you faced your dragons and did your best to slay them.

"Bring around two horses," James told a waiting footman, and the lad rushed off. She and James went outside to wait, and thankfully they didn't have to wait long.

Two grooms came into view outside with a pair of horses. Gillian spoke quickly to a footman she knew named Will.

"Tell Audrey everything that has happened. And apologize to his lordship for us taking his horses. We will see them returned as soon as possible."

"Of course. Be careful!" Will said and rushed back into the house.

Gillian mounted her horse with the aid of a groom, hitching her skirts high above her knees. Damn the consequences.

James mounted his and checked to see how Gillian was faring. "Ready?"

She nodded. "I'll keep up, I promise."

They rode at such a blinding pace that Gillian struggled to breathe. Dusk crept along the skies, stealing the light bit by bit. Gillian feared they would lose the light before they reached James's home, but luck prevailed. They rode along a gravel drive that led up to a beautiful castle. Early moonlight lit their way as she and James passed the gardens and halted at the stone steps that led up to a set of large oak wooden doors. Gillian slid out of her saddle, her legs and back aching with the hours in the saddle and the tension of the situation. A footman rushed out to meet them.

"Where is she?" James asked.

"The China room. Dr. Wilkes and Lady Letticia are with her."

James slipped past him into the hall. Gillian followed behind. She had but a moment to glimpse the beautiful world that James called home, the Flemish tapestries, the marble statues, and the thick oriental carpets. He was almost running as he reached the door and flung it open. Gillian was right behind him but froze at the sight of his mother lying in bed. Dr. Wilkes and Letty hovered nearby, both of them staring in surprise at her and James.

"You came." Letty choked out the words and rushed to embrace her brother.

Gillian's throat tightened, and she slipped back out into the hall. If he needed her, he would call for her, but she would not intrude on something so personal unless asked to. But she would wait for as long as he needed her to, and she would be there for him.

🥢 10 🥢

James knelt at his mother's side, clutching her hand. Her breath was shallow and her eyes glassy, but she turned her head his way when he came into the room.

"My boy." The words escaped her lips in a faint whisper.

"I'm here, Mother, I'm here." He brushed his knuckles over her cheek, feeling the fever that met his fingertips. His body and soul filled with a bone-deep dread.

"Where's your father?" his mother asked. "I want to see him."

James's heart bled. His mother still couldn't remember, couldn't move past that period of her life when his father had still been alive.

"He's—he's out hunting, Mother. I'm sure he'll be back shortly." For the hundredth time he wished that his father

155

really was out hunting, that he had never died. Another sob escaped Letty as she got down on her knees on her mother's other side and buried her face in the bedding.

"Letty," their mother murmured, stroking her hand over Letty's dark hair. "I think your father is late..." Lady Pembroke sounded amused, despite her fatigue. "Probably stopped to rest at the hunting lodge..." Her eyes suddenly brightened, and James clutched her hand tighter. "I should go and find him. Sometimes he likes it when I come to fetch him..." She smiled weakly, her eyes fixed on something he would never see, and then the light faded, her lids closed, and she peacefully slipped away.

James watched, his heart shattering as he stared at his mother. It looked as though she was merely sleeping.

Letty began to weep. Dr. Wilkes came over to the bed, lifting Lady Pembroke's wrist. Then after a moment he carefully set it back down and gave a heavy sigh.

"My lord, I'm so very sorry." Dr. Wilkes came over to him and placed a gentle hand on his shoulder. James could barely hold in the pain. He wanted to shout, to rage, to obliterate the silence around him. He stared hard at his mother's face, got to his feet, and pulled Letty to him. He gripped his sister tight, wishing he could absorb her pain into himself.

"It's all right," he said and kissed the crown of her hair. But it wouldn't be all right. They had lost their mother too early, just as they had their father. And he hadn't been there, hadn't been watching out for his mother. He had been at some silly house party.

When Letty finally quieted in his arms, she pulled back to look up at him, her eyes red and her face shining with tear streaks.

"James, I—" She bit her lip, holding back.

"Why don't you go to your rooms and rest. I will take care of Mother now," he promised.

She nodded, still shaking as she left the room. He turned to face Dr. Wilkes, his mind and heart blissfully numb for now. He would have to face his pain soon enough, but he needed to keep his composure for just a while longer.

⚜

GILLIAN TENSED AS LETTY EMERGED FROM THE ROOM. Their gazes locked.

"Is she...?"

"Yes." Letty sniffed, tears shining on her cheeks. "My brother promised he would take care of her."

"And he will. He loves you both so much." Gillian wanted to say something, anything that might help, but she knew by the look on Letty's face it wasn't the right thing.

Letty wiped her tears. "My mother has just died. Don't you think you owe my brother the truth about who you really are? If this is some game you're playing to get a title and money, I won't let you hurt James. Not after losing our mother."

"The truth?" Gillian echoed, her heart pounding on her ribs. Letty knew—somehow she had discovered who she really was. Dread knotted in her stomach.

"Yes. The *truth*. If you won't tell him who you really are, I will. And then you can explain to him what you really want and why you deceived him." Letty's warning lingered in the hall long after she rushed away.

Gillian pressed her back against the wall by the door. How had she discovered it?

After fifteen minutes, the door opened and James stepped into the corridor. He turned to her, and his eyes—those lovely brown eyes that filled her heart with love—were filled only with emptiness.

"Gillian..." He opened his arms, and she rushed to him, holding him tight.

Take my love, take my strength, she prayed.

James's body quaked against hers, like a solid stone house vibrating with the thunder of a distant storm.

"I'm sorry," he whispered brokenly. "I am—sorry, I can't—"

"Don't apologize. I'm here." She pressed a kiss to his neck, holding him to her.

A long while later, James wiped tears from his eyes. With a sad smile, he sighed. "I don't know how to thank you for coming with me today." He opened his hand to her, and she placed her palm in his.

"There's no need to thank me. I wanted to be here for you."

He drew a shaky breath. "It's so strange, but I feel a terrible relief that she's gone. I loved her greatly, with all my heart, but..." He struggled for words, and she didn't push him. "As she began to lose herself, bit by bit, day by day, as she vanished, I had already started to say goodbye. It was as though I had been prepared for this day years ago." He brushed his thumb over the back of her hand. "Does that sound mad?"

"No," Gillian said. "The most difficult thing we face as children is when we lose a parent. It's not easy to lose them without a goodbye, and yet it's harder still to know the end is coming and to feel you are losing them while they still draw breath. I wish I could do more to comfort you." She leaned into him again, hugging him fiercely, and he embraced her back. That single moment was something she would never forget, she and James standing together against a world that seemed determined to break their hearts at every turn.

This is why I love him, this strong, brave man who opened his heart to me. How could I not?

He kissed the crown of her hair, and they slowly broke apart. James cleared his throat, looking bashful. "I believe we could use some tea, and I need to write a letter to Lord Rochester explaining our abrupt departure."

He tried to keep himself composed; she could see that. He wanted to hide his pain and act normally even though his heart was broken. She would not force him to face his pain; he would do so in his own time.

"Do not worry about Lord Rochester. I left word with a footman as we were leaving. Why don't we find somewhere quiet to talk?" she suggested.

"Er—yes."

He took her to a beautiful blue and yellow drawing room where they sat by the fire, neither speaking for a long moment. Gillian took the time to memorize the way the light caught on his dark hair, revealing those hidden hues of warmth. His hands rested on his knees as he gazed unseeing into the flames.

"James, I know this is the worst moment for me to bring up such a matter, but..." She cleared her throat. "It's time you learn the truth about me. I want you to hear it from me, not anyone else." The last thing she wanted to do was add to his pain, but Letty would tell him if she did not.

"Gillian, you don't have to—"

She held up a hand. "I owe you the truth, James. From the moment we met in Madame Ella's modiste shop, I should have been honest with you."

He stared at her now, a look of worry in his eyes, as though he sensed that her confession would be the end.

"I'm not who you think I am. I wish with all my heart that I was, but I am not."

He tilted his head. "What do you mean? Don't speak in riddles."

"I—I'm not a lady. I am—" She had to draw a fortifying breath. She couldn't just say she was a lady's maid. That would make this so much worse. Instead she decided to explain in a less direct route. "My father was Lord Morrey."

His eyes widened. "Your...but...Morrey had a son and a daughter, Lord Adam Beaumont and Lady Caroline, his sister."

"I am the late Lord Morrey's daughter as well. He took a mistress after his wife passed." She waited, wondering if she would have to say it or if he would.

"You're illegitimate?"

She bit her lip, knowing she must continue. "After my father died, I had to support myself and my mother, but she died not long after my father, and I turned to service."

James cleared his throat. "By service, you mean—"

"I was, and still am, a lady's maid. To Audrey Sheridan."

His eyes were dark and fathomless, and he said nothing. Silence grew between them.

She cleared her throat and continued. "I never meant to deceive you. That day we first met at the modiste, I had been charged with trying on Miss Sheridan's latest order. The two of us are about the same size, and then you..." She couldn't continue, but it was clear in James's eyes that he pieced together how innocently the deception had begun. "I tried to stay away from you, but you pulled me back in like the sea pulls the shore."

There was never any stopping it once they met. She only now realized that the pull between them would *always* be there, at least for her, and she knew with a melancholy certainty that she would feel the tug of her heart every day that she had to live without him.

"A lady's maid." He stared at her, his face expressionless.

He's furious. He has to be. I deceived him. How could he not despise me?

She raised her chin a little, trying everything to keep from crying. "Yes. Do you wish for me to leave?"

"Leave?" He blinked as though he was waking from a trance. "Gillian, I love you. The last thing I would ever want is for you to leave, but..."

But... How that single word burned like an awful fire in her heart.

"But," he continued, his voice still hoarse with emotion, "my mother has just passed, and while I would marry you tomorrow, I must see to funeral arrangements, and we must delay for the proper length of time. Mourning must be observed. People will gossip enough as it is, but if we wait, it will help."

This time it was Gillian who blinked. "You want to marry me?"

"Of course." He stood, paced to the fireplace, and then walked back.

"But you can't. I'm not even a gentleman's daughter." It was his grief talking, looking desperately to cling to something or someone. He did not mean to marry her—he couldn't. It was madness; it was unacceptable.

"You're the daughter of an earl."

"I'm the *bastard* daughter of an earl," she countered.

He leaned down to cup her face in his hands, smiling a little.

"My darling. My love. It never mattered who you *thought* you were. What matters is who I *know* you to be."

She trembled beneath his touch as he stroked the pad of his thumb over her lips, his eyes searching hers. "And who is that?"

"The woman of my heart. I've never felt like this with anyone else. Only with you. I will fight the world to be with you if I must. I faced hellfire clubs and devil cats to be with you. Do you honestly think I would let *society* stand in my way?"

"But I cannot be the one to destroy your reputation. You are not thinking clearly." She curled her fingers around his wrists, clinging to him when she knew she should be letting go.

He lowered his head to hers, brushing her lips in a kiss that sent singing notes of music through her soul. But she was too afraid to embrace this joy. Her life was never meant to be one of happiness. Not like this.

"I must send you back to Rochester's house."

And there it was, the decision to let her go.

"Of course. I understand," she whispered, her lashes

lowering as she fought off tears. "It's the right thing to do."

"Gillian," he growled. "Look at me."

She did so.

"I must send you home to your mistress so that you have time to prepare a proper trousseau. You must inform her of your resignation from her employment. I trust she will not be angry that I'm stealing you away?"

Gillian still couldn't believe she was hearing this, that he wanted her, even after knowing the truth.

"She will be upset to lose me, but happy too. She knows how I feel about you."

James lifted her to her feet and pulled her into his arms. "She'd better be. She was the one who invited me to the party, after all."

"What?" Gillian gasped. "But she said she didn't." Well, actually she hadn't, but she'd seemed genuinely surprise at James coming to Rochester's house party.

"I came to the Sheridan townhouse last week before the party, the morning after the hellfire club incident."

"I remember," Gillian confessed. "I was hiding in the servants' entrance and saw you come in."

He rubbed his hands up and down her back. "So close, and yet I'd no idea you were there."

"Why did you come that day?" she asked.

"To find you. Miss Sheridan was the only connection I had to you. I begged her to tell me where you were, *who* you were. She didn't betray your identity, but she said I could come to the party and win you over."

Gillian shook her head in disbelief. Until this moment Gillian had believed Audrey's ambition of being a spy was a fool's errand, but now she was beginning to think she might be clever enough to fool the king of France.

"Indeed." James threaded his fingers through her hair kissed her, a torrent of passion pouring from his lips. When their mouths finally parted, he pressed his forehead to hers. The sorrow returned to his eyes, and he squeezed her in a fierce hug as though only she could comfort him.

"You'll wait for me? I need to focus on arranging the funeral."

"If you truly want me, I will wait for you however long you need," she vowed.

If James was willing to brave the condemnation of society for her, she would do everything she could to be worthy of him, even if she had to wait forever.

Two weeks had passed since James's mother had died, yet he still felt her presence in the townhouse after he and Letty returned to London. He missed her with every breath, yet a part of him felt relieved that she was no longer suffering. She'd not been herself for several years, and he'd wished that if he could not have healed her, he could at least have her pain ended. While his heart was still broken, he knew that she was with his father now, and there, together, they could be happy.

James lingered in the entry hall, hat in hand as he prepared himself for the day that would forever change his life. He was going to go and claim Gillian as his own. Publicly, in the manner she deserved. He knew she had promised to wait, and they had written to each other every day reaffirming their commitment, yet his stomach was tight with knots.

"James..." His sister's voice made him turn. Letty descended the stairs, looking rather lovely in a simple lilac day gown proper for mourning and a shawl. It was the usual time of day for her to call upon her friends but given their mother's death she was remaining at home for the next several months.

"Ah, Letty, I'm glad you're here. I need to speak with you." He hadn't officially told his sister yet that he intended to marry Gillian. Part of him feared she would be angry with him over the match. Ever since she'd discovered Gillian's history, her manner had seemed oddly strained whenever he mentioned her name in conversation.

"And I need to say a few things as well." She reached him at the bottom of the stairs. Pain and worry was so clear in her eyes that his breath caught. This did not bode well.

"Letty, what—"

"Please, let me speak first," she begged.

James nodded, his body now tight with anxiety.

"I forced Gillian to tell you the truth about her circumstances. You see, I visited her half brother, Lord Morrey, and it turns out he's been searching for her ever since their father died. He wants to know her, to support her. He's not ashamed of the connection at all." She sighed, her lips curving slightly. "He's quite wonderful, actually. But I was upset, and I fear I made a mess of things. When Mama passed, I was hurting terribly, and I saw her and..." His sister paused, sniffled, and continued. "I feared the worst about her intentions. I told her that she must confess her situation to you, or I would."

James didn't know what to say, but he wasn't angry. He understood Letty's pain and the need to lash out. He might have reacted that way, but he hadn't. Gillian had been there for him. She'd done something he'd never thought possible: she'd taken part of his grief and carried it upon her own shoulders. Her strength and support had made the loss more bearable. At the time he'd felt guilty about sharing that burden, but then he'd realized something that filled his heart with hope. When you met the person who was destined to be your life partner, you couldn't force pain upon them—they took it willingly from you, and they shared it. He could never have hidden his heart from Gillian, because it belonged to her. She would always see him when he was at his darkest, at his most wounded, and she would be there to help. Not because she had to, but because she wanted to.

And I will do the same for her. Every hurt, every joy, everything, we will share together.

"Letty, please, don't be upset. I'm not angry with you," he said. He cupped her chin and lifted her face, hating the tears that coated her lashes.

"You're not?"

"No. But I must tell you something now and hear the

truth from you. It is my intention to marry Gillian. Will that cause you any further pain?"

Letty shook her head. "I always liked her, you know that. I only wanted to protect you. So many women long for a title, and I feared someone would take advantage of your open heart."

James gave a gentle laugh. "You've always been fierce in matters of the heart, and I admire you for it. But rest assured, I shall be well so long as I have Gillian."

"Then I am glad." Letty's smile was bright like the sun. Whoever married her someday would cherish such smiles.

"I'm off to visit her. Would you care to come?"

"No, but give her my love when you see her. It will be such a joy to have her here once you are married."

"Do you mean that?" James settled his hat upon his head and pulled on his riding gloves.

"Of course," Letty assured him. "Now off with you! I know you're anxious to see her." Letty shoved him toward the door. He couldn't help but smile. He was indeed anxious for the rest of his wonderful life with Gillian to begin.

🐾

AUDREY RUSHED INTO THE DRAWING ROOM. "HE'S here!"

Gillian sat up and tossed aside the embroidery hoop she had been pretending to care about. In truth, she'd been sticking the same piece over and over again since a messenger had informed her that James was coming to formally ask for her hand. She could scarcely believe it'd been two weeks, yet the days had seemed to both drag on and pass too quickly without her being able to see him.

Cedric, Audrey's older brother, sat in a chair by the fire and folded his paper. He looked to Gillian.

"You're sure you want to marry him? I like the fellow immensely, of course, but you say the word and I will chase him off." Cedric smiled at her in a way that made her heart tremble with joy. He had taken over the situation at once when Gillian had been forced to explain her resignation. He'd changed from employer to honorary brother in a heartbeat. The Sheridans had always treated her like family, and now she felt more than ever that she was a part of it.

"Don't you dare!" Audrey said, slapping her brother's arm.

"My lord," Sean Hartley said as he appeared in the doorway. "There's a Lord Pembroke and a Lord Morrey here to see you both, and Miss Beaumont, of course."

Gillian's throat constricted, and she had to fight to remain calm. "Did you say Lord Morrey?"

Audrey looked her way, paling. "You said he didn't know about you."

"He didn't," Gillian said. What could all this mean?

"Do you still wish for me to let them in?" Sean asked.

Cedric studied Gillian. "It's up to you, my dear."

"I... Yes, let them in." She would simply have to face the situation and pray that Lord Morrey wasn't here to ruin her chance at happiness. She had done her best to remain invisible, to avoid drawing any attention to Lord Morrey's family. Once she was married, even her name would change. What more could she do?

Gillian remained standing, heart pounding, as she heard voices echo in the hall. Sean opened the door, and James entered first. His reassuring smile alleviated her worry, but only for a moment. The second gentleman, Lord Morrey, was tall, dark-haired, and had the same silvery dove-gray eyes that were not often seen in London. *We have the same eyes, just like our father.* He was handsome, elegant, yet a masculine specimen who would have sent her mistress swooning if she hadn't already been besotted with Jonathan St. Laurent.

"Lord Pembroke, Lord Morrey," Cedric greeted.

"Lord Sheridan," they both answered politely.

"Gillian, do you wish for me to remain? Or I shall I retire to my study? When Lord Pembroke and Lord Morrey are ready, they may discuss your dowry with me."

"Dowry?" Gillian was confused. "I have no dowry."

"Nonsense," Cedric said. "I shall provide one for you."

"Actually..." Lord Morrey cleared his throat, his expression unreadable. "I believe that is my duty, as next of kin."

Cedric crossed his arms. "You are here to acknowledge that she is a relation, then?"

"I am," Morrey said, frowning back at Cedric. "Insofar

as I am able. I hope no one is under the impression that I intended to disown her."

"Well," Cedric began, "it makes a man wonder. She's been in service all these years. Where were you when she needed help?"

"My lord!" Gillian blushed to the roots of her hair as she watched Cedric defend her. It wasn't necessary.

"You misunderstand. I have been searching for her," Morrey said to Cedric, then faced Gillian. "For quite some time now. My father, *our* father, wished for me to take care of you and your mother. I'm sorry that I failed to find you after he died, but I wish to make up for that now and do all that I can to help you." He was smiling, but there was a sadness to it. "It seems I'm too late, however. Lord Pembroke has informed me you two are to be wed. So the least I can do is give you a dowry and offer myself and my sister as your family."

"But..." The world suddenly tilted around her, and she gripped the back of the nearest chair to stay on her feet. James was there in an instant, catching her by the waist.

"Thank you."

"Of course," he whispered back.

"Lord Morrey, if you acknowledge any connection to me, it will cause a scandal."

Morrey grinned, lending a boyish glint in his all too serious eyes. "Ah, but I have thought of that. James mentioned your concern for scandal, and I believe we may have come up with a delightful solution. Haven't we, Pembroke?"

"I believe so." James glanced toward Audrey. "Ambrose Worthing, a friend of mine, was once able to enlist the aid of Lady Society. It is my hope to do the same."

Gillian saw Audrey suddenly stiffen.

"Lady Society?" Cedric chuckled. "You'd be better off making a deal with the devil. You'll be up to your neck in trouble with that woman, whoever she is."

"I don't think so," James said. "Lady Society is quite clever and has always championed matters of the heart, especially those that fly in the face of convention. She reminds her readers that we must temper our traditions with compassion."

"She also has a way of ferreting out the most inconvenient secrets and shining a light on them for all to see," Cedric countered. "I tell you, you are playing with fire if you hope to enlist her aid."

"She would be worth any price if she can assist me in convincing society to applaud rather than condemn my marriage to Gillian. I think she would agree it is a cause worth championing."

Gillian relaxed when she realized he wouldn't reveal Audrey's secret identity in front of her brother.

"What is your solution?" Cedric pressed.

Morrey was still smiling. "We will contact Lady Society through the *Quizzing Glass Gazette*, informing her of our situation and asking her aid. It is our hope that Lady

Society will write about the enchanting new lady in London, Miss Gillian Beaumont, rumored to be a cousin from the country, an old family connection that my sister and I are excited to renew. Of course, if she believes she has a more effective means of reaching the public, we will defer to her expertise."

"Your sister does not object?" Gillian asked, holding her breath.

"Of course not. I hope you are open to us as well... sister," Morrey said, and the tenderness in his tone shocked her. For a moment Gillian couldn't breathe. A joy so strong seemed to burst inside her that she had to calm herself lest she burst into tears. She'd expected Morrey to want to pay her off to hide her, to discredit her, or ignore her at the very least. But to welcome her so openly? It was beyond anything she'd ever dreamed.

"Thank you, my lord," she said, her eyes misting.

Morrey was still watching her closely, his warm smile growing at her response. "You'll find us to be worthy siblings. Father taught us that family matters, and you are a part of ours."

Cedric beamed. "Well said! Glad to hear you got the right of it, Morrey."

Morrey approached Gillian and held out a hand. "I know you have no need of my blessing to marry Pembroke, but you have it, along with a healthy dowry."

"I truly don't need it," James said. "Gillian's heart is all I truly need."

"Please. Allow me to provide it so that you may shower your wife with gifts. After all her years in service, I believe she deserves nothing less," Morrey insisted.

Shower her with gifts? The thought was so foreign it was laughable.

"What do you think, love?" James asked. "The best gowns, the finest slippers, an entire room for just your bonnets?"

"Yes! Of course she wants that!" Audrey exclaimed. "Gillian, you're going to have a room for your very own bonnets!" Her friend's eyes glowed with mischief and sheer joy at the thought of all those silly hats being piled in one room.

Gillian sighed and chuckled. "Perhaps we might extend the library to include more novels instead?"

James grinned at her. "Novels it is, but I do insist on the gowns and slippers at least."

She bit her lip. "Because I'm so very plain?"

James stared at her in astonishment. "Far from it! You're the loveliest woman I've ever met. But I wish to provide you with the best to make every woman jealous."

"Oh." It would certainly take getting used to, the idea of anyone being jealous of her.

"So all that is left is to choose a date, then?" James asked. "Would Christmas suit you?"

"Is that too soon after your mother's passing?"

James shook his head. "Officially yes, which means people will talk, I'm sure, but I'm a bachelor, quite a catch, or so I am told, so it won't surprise them that I've been snapped up. What's the point in waiting? I told you I didn't mind scandal" Humor glinted in his eyes as he curled an arm around her waist.

"Christmas would be wonderful, then." She tilted her face up to his, basking in the sunniness of his smile.

James stole a quick kiss. Cedric and Morrey both harrumphed strongly, but more for propriety's sake than any actual objection.

"I shall come to call for tea, riding on Rotten Row..." He pressed a lingering kiss to her hand. "You will be courted properly, just as I promised."

Gillian's heart was suddenly so completely full of love, a joy so overpowering she could scarcely stand it. In a matter of weeks, she'd gone from an orphaned servant to a lady with two protective brothers.

"See? I promised you good things would come after we met all those years ago," Audrey said with a twinkle in her eyes. "Very good things."

Gillian smiled at her friend and mouthed the words that could never fully relay the depth of her gratitude. *Thank you.*

"That's what sisters are for," Audrey said. She shrugged as if giving her such joy had been a simple duty and not the greatest gift anyone could ever receive. Lady Society could indeed work miracles. She had given Gillian a love like no other, a man who truly cared about her, someone who wanted her as a partner in life.

James was watching her, that look of hope still in his eyes, but there was something more. Not just hope, but a promise of love and a life together. He was her wonderful, wicked earl, after all, and he would make her every dream come true.

EPILOGUE

ne month later

Gillian stood in the dining room of James's townhouse, her wedding gown whispering on the carpets as she walked around the long table. The guests would be arriving any minute from the church to attend the breakfast feast, but she had a few precious moments alone to admire the cook's creations. The table was laden with cakes and other delicacies, and there was an abundance of orange flowers that filed the air with their scent, making the room feel more like a garden. For so long she had been on the other side of this kind of life, the one who must be unseen and unheard, toiling away in the predawn hours and late into the night to make another person's life better. Now she was the one who would have anything she wished. It was strange rather than comforting to think about, and she knew it would take some getting used to being a lady rather than a lady's maid.

"Gillian?" Gillian turned to see her new sister-in-law standing in the doorway.

"Yes?" She studied Letty as she walked over. Her brown eyes were solemn and remorseful.

"In all the madness of the quick wedding, I never had a chance to apologize." Letty reached out to touch Gillian's hands. "I never should have pushed you to tell James about your past, not that day. It was wrong of me, and I'm sorry if I accused you of trying to deceive him for selfish reasons." Letty's voice broke slightly.

"Letty, there's nothing to forgive. You were protecting him. I would expect nothing less from a devoted sister." She still clasped the other woman's hands in hers.

"But I hate the true reasons behind my actions. I was more self-serving than I led you to believe. I was afraid of the scandal as well. But if I've learned anything from you, it's that scandal doesn't matter, not when it comes to love. I liked you from the first moment we met, and I shouldn't have tried to come between you and James. You make him so happy, wonderfully so, and he deserves that happiness more than any man I know. You're the perfect woman for him, no matter where you came from or who you once were. What matters is who you are—the woman he loves, the woman who makes him happy."

Indeed, how true that is, Gillian thought with a small

smile. She and James had planned to wed around Christmas, but she had missed her menses only two weeks after being engaged, and they decided not to risk talk in the *ton* in order to protect the child she was quite sure she carried. There had been a storm of whispers at the first few dinners she had attended, and many ladies had been upset that James was no longer a bachelor. He found it rather amusing, and soon Gillian had relaxed, once she was positive the gossips weren't harming him or his sister. In fact, the intervention of Lady Society had helped, just as he and Adam had hoped.

Audrey had penned a delightful article about Gillian, which most of the ton seemed convinced by. The whispers around her had been mostly about her mysteriousness and her quiet beauty and natural grace than they were speculation as to her familial circumstances. And Gillian could not forget how quickly she'd been welcomed by her half brother, Adam, and her half sister, Caroline, as family.

"I'm so happy you're a part of our family," Letty added. "That day I met you at the modiste's shop, I had a feeling about you. A sense of kindred spirits." Her eyes shone with tears of happiness, and then she hugged Gillian.

"Thank you! I never imagined I would gain two sisters in one month, but I'm so glad we are family now."

"Agreed! It's so much fun to have a sister in the house." Letty squeezed her again, smiling. "I have to go find my brother. The guests will be here soon."

She left Gillian alone again in the dining room. She reached out to touch the delicately made porcelain pitchers. The colorful china patterns of red and gold flowers reminded her of James and the long rides they liked to take in Hyde Park as they watched the leaves turn to gold. All around her, life was beautiful, and her future shone like a bright star in the winter sky.

"Trying to steal a bit of cake?" James's teasing tone made her smile. He entered the dining room, looking fine in his black jacket, waistcoat, and tan trousers. His brown eyes gleamed like hot chocolate.

"I admit, I am tempted. The idea that I already eat for two is a bit daunting." She placed a palm over her still-flat belly. She hadn't forgotten Horatia's difficult labor or how frightened everyone had been. James came over, curling his arms around her waist and pulling her flush against him. Their faces were mere inches apart. They shared the same breath, eyes locked upon each other.

"We'll face it together. Anything that frightens you, I will be at your side." His vow was whispered in a soft voice, yet with the conviction of a knight of ages past, vowing to protect his lady fair. As much as Gillian insisted she'd never needed rescuing, knowing that he would fight for her gave her a new kind of strength. She knew her own virtues because she'd supported herself for so many years, but knowing she had a partner at her side made a world of difference to her. They could face anything together.

"Do I truly make you happy?" she asked as she toyed

with the folds of his snowy-white cravat. She supposed it would take a while to banish the fears that she wasn't enough for him. A lifetime of doubts did not vanish overnight.

There were no shadows in his eyes as he cupped her cheek. "There has only ever been joy for me when I'm with you. When you're here, it's like feeling the sun on my face after a cold winter. You breathed *life* into me. No one has ever come close to making me feel that way. No other name will fill my heart but yours." His eyes burned with startling intensity. "What must I do to prove you're the only one for me?"

There was nothing he could do. He'd already proven it time and again.

She swallowed. "I simply cannot believe that fate would give you to me. That I am worthy of such a gift." She leaned her face into his hand, closing her eyes and drawing in a slow breath. "For so long I dared not to dream, dared not to believe I could have a full life, one of joy and love. I feared I would always be on the outside of a window looking in at a world that could never be mine. How can I possibly deserve you and all of this?" She gestured to the beautifully decorated dining room, but she referred to so much more.

"Everyone deserves love and a good life," James said "You and I were simply luckier than most to find ours together."

He lowered his head, his mouth covering hers in a

heated kiss. She imagined she could get drunk on such a taste, on his arms holding her tight and the feel of his heart beating so close to her own. Her once-tired soul had been roused by the passion and ferocity of his love. She smiled as she remembered that day a month ago when they had spoken John Donne's poem "The Good Morrow" together:

IF OUR TWO LOVES BE ONE, OR, THOU AND I
  Love so alike, that none do slacken, none can die.

EVERY WORD OF IT HAD BEEN TRUE THEN, AND IT would remain so always.

Wait! This isn't the end...I know you were panicking there for a minute right? Don't worry, the League will continue! The best way to know when Jonathan, Charles and the rest of the League and their friends are released is to do one or all of the following:

Join my Newsletter: http://laurensmithbooks.com/ free-books-and-newsletter/

Follow Me on BookBub: https://www.bookbub.com/ authors/lauren-smith

Join my Facebook VIP Reader Group called Lauren Smith's League: https://www.facebook.com/ groups/400377546765661/

THE NEXT BOOK IN THE SERIES IS *HIS WICKED Secret*, the story of Jonathan and Audrey!

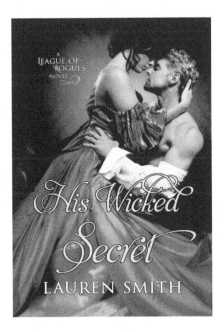

IF YOU'D LIKE TO READ THE PROLOGUE AND FIRST chapter from the next book in the Wicked Earls' Series *The Earl of Seville* by Christina McKnight just turn the page!

EARL OF ST. SEVILLE

BY CHRISTINA MCKNIGHT

P rologue
January 1822
London, England

JAMES LANE, THE EARL OF DESMOND, STROLLED DOWN the darkened lane bordering Covent Garden without benefit of the gaslights that were commonplace in the more civilized areas of London. Pall Mall, Oxford Street, Bond Street, and even Savile Row in Mayfair. The earl pulled at the lapel of his coat to keep the crisp evening air from sending wave after wave of shivers through him. He wasn't as young as he'd once been, nor was he as strong or confident as the young lord who'd claimed the love of Ivory Bess not far from this very spot.

The clip of horses' hooves sounded behind Desmond,

reminding him that losing focus and letting his guard down in such a neighborhood—and so late into the night—could mean his death. He glanced over his shoulder. No one followed as he hurried toward his carriage, halted at the end of the street—only four dark and abandoned buildings away —his driver idly passing the time huddled in his thick, wool coat on his perch where Desmond had left him two hours prior. His footman kept watch near the boot of the carriage.

Despite his advanced age and the frigid January weather, the earl continued to visit London's more dubious neighborhoods.

Even with the love of his life taken from him five years ago, Desmond came. There was a day when he'd thought his life ended with her. His countess, the mother of his children, the love of his life was gone from him. However, Ivory "Bess" Lane, the Countess of Desmond, his wife and soul mate, had left a piece of herself in each of their children, Patience especially.

It was for his youngest daughter, Lady Patience Lane, that Desmond risked his safety night after night when he journeyed round London, entering various gaming hells and taverns.

If it weren't for Patience, Desmond would have retired to his country estate in Somerset to live out his days surrounded by things that reminded him of his Ivory— their many good years together before the trials of her youth came back to haunt her.

Yet, retiring to a life of solitude in the English country-side was not to be...

"More's the pity," he mumbled into the night.

Desmond would have his time to grieve once all his daughters were happily wed. His sons would find their own way, just as Desmond had after he left University.

Two down, and only Patience left unattached—sadly with no prospects on the horizon.

Shoving his gloved hands deep into his greatcoat pockets, his fingers wrapped around the newly printed pamphlets he'd come to Covent Gardens to distribute. He knew it was a lost cause, but it meant something to Patience.

Ironically, distributing Patience's precisely crafted pamphlets also decreased her chances of finding a suitable match even more.

The men—and many women—who gained their living stripped down to the waist with their bare knuckles raised and poised to fight were not interested in learning about the risks of their pugilist pursuits. Damnation, many of them couldn't so much as read the pamphlets Patience painstakingly created. They were not interested in the injuries and damage caused by repeated blows to the head and torso; they were more concerned with earning the coin to pay for food and shelter. A livelihood for themselves and their families.

Many in London had no other means but what could

be gained by using their brute strength, sure fists, and light feet.

Be that as it may, he continued to indulge Patience. He'd never tell her that her hard work littered the floors of gaming hells as men readily discarded the papers as rubbish, or was used to wipe down grimy windows. She never journeyed to any of the hells and taverns and so never knew the fate of her pamphlets.

Desmond had slowed as he allowed his mind to wander.

Another sign he had become overly lax during his nighttime trips across London.

Keeping his eyes on his driver perched on the seat of his waiting coach, Desmond increased his pace, ready to escape to the solitude of his study.

With only two buildings separating him from that fate, the earl passed an alley littered with debris and spoiled table scraps—where two men could be seen embroiled in a scuffle.

He ought to avert his gaze and keep walking.

What transpired in the dark lane between two grown men was none of his business and could lead to Desmond being injured or even killed. It would do his children little good if he got himself stabbed for interfering in something that was not his concern.

Yet, he stared into the alley as the men tussled, knocking one another to the ground.

Haphazardly hung fabric in the windows of the tenements were pulled back as the people living above the alley stared down at the spectacle, the candlelight from their open windows casting a glow around the two men. Twenty years ago—perhaps as few as ten—Desmond wouldn't have hesitated to separate the two men before anyone was grievously injured.

But now, he had less time to live—and so much more he needed to see done before he left this life.

Another tenant in the building above pulled back what appeared to be undergarments strung on a line for drying, sending more muted light through the grimy windowpane and directly down on the skirmish below.

One of the men was outfitted as most were in the Covent Garden district: loose trousers and a long, hole-ridden tunic with shoes years past needing mending by a cobbler. However, the other opponent could not be mistaken for anything but gentry, if not a lord like Desmond. As the fighters regained their footing, the earl noticed that the nobleman's sheer size nearly filled the alley from stone wall to stone wall, his height as impressive as his stature. His hair, hanging past his shoulders in golden brown waves, was the only hint that mayhap he was not among London's elite *ton*, for what man—except highwaymen and pirates—allowed his hair to fall down his back at such a length? For a brief second, the light reflected off highly polished Hessians as the massive Corinthian sidestepped a fist, causing the smaller man to list forward and slam into the stone wall as his balance fled him.

"Come 'ere, ya toff," the man called, turning away from the building and raising his fists in preparation for another assault.

Desmond wasn't certain how the finely dressed man had wandered down this particular street, but a thief had obviously set upon him. Perhaps he'd been visiting one of the various gaming hells situated several streets over.

The ruffian threw another jab, catching the larger man in the mouth.

The gentleman needed assistance. Despite Desmond's age and frailty, he was the man's only option this far into the alley, no longer in view of Desmond's carriage and driver. If the earl screamed for help, would his driver come running? Desmond would never forgive himself if injury came to his servant as a direct result of his call for help.

Glancing around, Desmond spotted a long, wooden handle, likely discarded when the hammer portion broke from the end, making the tool useless except as fire kindling.

It would do the job needing done. He only needed to create enough of a distraction for the gentleman—and himself—to escape the alley and flee to the waiting coach.

Desmond took hold of the wooden rod and advanced farther into the dim alley as the ruffian, his trousers as threadbare as his tunic, swiftly jabbed his fist, pummeling the other man in the chest. The fighters shuffled their feet, clench fists raised as they hopped in a tight circle, each looking for another opportunity to strike out at the other.

It was a scene Desmond was all too familiar with.

The exact occurrence that Patience's painstakingly crafted pamphlets hoped to discourage.

Desmond inched closer and bided his time. He waited for the men to move so that he could club the lout with enough force to halt the attack. If Desmond struck at the correct time, he and the other gentleman could depart the alley without further confrontation.

Finally, the moment presented itself, and Desmond swung the thick stick with enough force to nick the man's shoulder and send him reeling to the muck-strewn dirt.

The Corinthian paused, his eyes darting to Desmond and back to his assailant as he moved to regain his feet.

"I think it best we leave," Desmond called, discarding the club against the alley wall out of reach of the ruffian, the sound echoing in the alley. "Let us be off."

When the gentleman made no move to follow him, Desmond wondered if he'd made a grave mistake by assuming that the henchman was the aggressor in the situation.

The smaller man regained his footing quicker than Desmond anticipated, though only grabbed the gentleman's coat where he'd discarded it on a stack of crates against the alley wall. He fled deeper into the dark passageway, disappearing from sight, his footfalls echoing in the wake of his escape.

Neither Desmond nor the other man moved in pursuit.

"My carriage is down the street," Desmond said, nodding toward the mouth of the alley. "Your lip is split and may need stitches to mend properly. Come, I will have my personal physician tend to your wounds."

"The chap stole my overcoat," the man breathed, his hands resting on his hips as he sucked air in deep, wincing slightly. The cut on his lip most certainly stung when the night air hit it.

Desmond wanted to chuckle. "At least you are escaping with your life and no new holes on your person."

He remembered being young and impulsive—exhilarated at the thought of a skilled match against an accomplished pugilist.

Again, Desmond wondered if the man needed saving to begin with.

In that moment, Patience came to mind; her single-minded determination to warn fighters about the peril they faced when they accepted the challenge of a worthy competitor. Lost memories, unending bouts of lethargy, headaches, and vision impairment.

His Ivory Bess, once a prized pugilist in her own right, had suffered more than most with all those ailments.

Desmond narrowed his glare at the man, tilting his chin up to focus on the gentleman's face and not his chest. "We should go, in case the man decides to return."

"I can find my own way back to my lodging."

"I'm not certain you even know where you are, my friend," Desmond retorted. The maze of alleyways and lanes that crisscrossed London were difficult to navigate, and even more daunting in the dark.

Candles extinguished as the residents of the building overlooking the alley lost interest in the scene below. With their departure, the meager light that had shone down on the filthy passageway disappeared, shrouding Desmond in shadows as unease rose the hairs on the back of his neck.

Desmond turned, waving for the man to follow. "My coach is this way."

Exiting the alleyway, the earl curved right and was reassured to see his coach and driver waiting. A sharp whistle garnered the driver's attention, and his servant leapt down from his perch and whisked the door open, not bothering to set down the steps.

Desmond took the forward-facing seat, surprised to note that the stranger alighted directly after him, taking the seat across from him.

"My townhouse," he called as his driver closed the door.

"Right away, my lord."

The carriage shifted, and the creak of the brake lever broke the silence in the confined space as the horses were called into action.

"My lodging is at the Albany." The man's deep voice reverberated off the walls of the coach. "I will be forever grateful and in your debt if you can deposit me there."

He was definitely of noble birth, as further evidenced by his cultured tone.

Desmond scoffed. "There is no physician in residence near the Albany at this time of night. My doctor will see to your wounds, and I will arrange for transport back to the Albany after."

The grim set of the man's frown told Desmond that he was not used to answering to another.

That made two of them.

Besides his three hellion daughters, Desmond's edicts were taken as strict orders, and no one in his household disobeyed his command.

"Your name, my boy?" Desmond took in the almost unbelievable width of the man's shoulders and the sharp edge of his jawline. He was at least twenty years Desmond's junior, if not more. And the earl recognized the rebellious light in his eyes all too well.

Reluctantly, the man answered, "Sinclair Chambers— err, Earl of St. Seville. And who shall I commend as my guardian angel?"

"The Earl of Desmond, James to my closest friends." He eyed the man across from him, St. Seville's dark eyes appearing black in the dim interior of the coach. "St. Seville, you say. Of the Brownsea Island St. Sevilles?"

St. Seville's brooding mask of irritation transformed to utter shock. "Yes, you know of my family?"

"Your father is—err, *was*—Ellis Chambers?"

"Correct." St. Seville crossed his arms over his chest, and a new guarded mask hooded his expression. "Were you acquainted?"

Desmond could barely believe his eyes. If he looked closely at the young man across from him, he noted the hardened jawline and severe nose with a mouth that appeared more of a slash across his face that was so characteristic of the St. Seville family, even with his split lip that now boasted a patch of drying red blood. Even if the man seated facing Desmond were twice the size of his predecessor, the earl could see the family resemblance as clear as if they stood under a bright June sun with the men side by side. Desmond hadn't seen the elder St. Seville in over two decades. He'd nearly forgotten the man's existence.

"Ellis and I were once close—both members of The Earls' Guild here in London—however, he left town shortly after his wedding and retired to his family estate. If you have taken the title, I assume your father has passed. When did it happen?"

"Going on four years now." St. Seville glanced at the window, pulling aside the cloth covering the glass insert. "My mother and sister remain on the island."

Four years, and word hadn't reached Desmond.

To be fair, his mind had been occupied with his own

sorrows. Five long years since his wife had left him alone, and it was still all Desmond thought of.

"I am sorry for your loss," Desmond sighed. "Ellis was a good man."

A snort was the younger man's only reply as the carriage pulled to a halt.

"I can see myself back to the Albany and take care of my own needs, my lord." His gruff reply had Desmond wondering if he remembered Ellis incorrectly.

"I am afraid I must insist on seeing to your care. It is the least I can do for my old friend, your father." Desmond held St. Seville's weary glare as his driver opened the door to allow them exit. "We lost touch all those years ago, and I fear it was my duty to remain in contact. Please, allow my physician to see to your injuries. It would do much to assuage an old man's guilt."

Desmond saw the moment the man acquiesced; his stiff shoulders sagged a bit, and he nodded.

CHAPTER 1

C hapter One
The familiar creak of a window opening in the room next door startled Lady Patience Lane from her deep slumber as a tremor of fear rolled through her. A chill ran up her spine despite the warmth of her room. Rubbing at her sleep-heavy eyes, she stretched her legs toward the cooled coals at the end of her bed as she sat up and listened. She tuned her hearing to any sound that did not belong.

Marsh Manor, the name her mother had christened their family townhouse with upon her marriage to her father, had been an unusually silent home in recent years. No longer did the structure ache and groan as it settled, no doors opened and closed in the night, and no window-pane was ever cracked during the bitter cold of winter despite the three other bordering buildings that blocked the worst of the late January wind.

Merit's room lay next door to Patience's, but the bedchamber had been empty for nearly two weeks, seeing that her brothers—Merit and Valor—had fled the dreary London weather for a holiday party near the Scottish border. Both of her sisters were happily wed and residing with their husbands, and they hardly visited unless her father commanded it. Besides her father and the Desmond servants, Patience was alone in the townhouse. Certainly, no servant had been tasked to clean Merit's room this late at night. The Desmond household didn't always stand on formalities, so when Patience and her father retired for the evening, so too did their staff.

When no other odd noises broke the silence of the night, Patience wondered if she hadn't imagined the entire thing and relaxed back into her soft, feather-filled bed. She pulled her covers high to her chin and closed her eyes, willing herself back to slumber.

Thump.

Patience sat bolt upright in bed, clutching her warm blankets to her chest as her wide-eyed stare darted around her dark room. The faint glow of the embers in her hearth told her that the hour was late, and the entire household was likely abed, despite the lingering warmth in her chambers.

Yet, *someone* was indeed in Merit's room.

Perhaps her brothers had returned early from their holiday.

The sound of a cough echoed through the thin wall, followed by a groan, and then another cough. An ensuing litany of cursing echoed, too low for Patience to comprehend every word but enough to fill her with a burst of happiness.

Her rascal of a brother *had* returned...and without the foresight of sending word to her.

Had he stopped at his club for a drink—or three—before arriving home? Perhaps that explained his less than subtle arrival and his string of highly unacceptable language.

None of that mattered. Her brother was home. Patience would no longer suffer through endless days of solitude with little conversation besides what she engaged in with her father or her maid.

Patience tossed her blankets aside and scurried from the sanctuary of her bed, her bare feet touching the cold, wood-planked floors as she hopped across the room in delight. Her unease from a few moments before was all but forgotten in her haste to chastise her brother for his untimely arrival, thus rousing her from sleep.

She wasn't actually vexed—quite the contrary in fact.

In truth, she missed her siblings greatly when they were not at home.

With her eldest sisters—Verity and Temperance—lovingly wed and living with their husbands, Patience found herself alone much of the time, her father hidden in his study claiming he had much work to do and could not be bothered by her idle chatter. Patience did not, in any way, see her discussions and debates regarding the health and safety of all her countrymen as idle *or* chatter. However, in addition to passing around her pamphlets, her father had begged her to set her attention on other topics.

That only left Valor and Merit to keep her company and banish the loneliness that had set in after their mother's passing five years prior.

Patience pulled her door open just enough to slip into the corridor, a draft ruffling the hem of her long, white nightshift around her bare ankles.

Indeed! A dim glow shone below her brother's door.

The eagerness that coursed through her was unexpected, though welcome. Except for her work crafting her pamphlets, Patience had little to occupy the long hours in each day, though she had taken her father's advice and researched drought in the Southern African nations and the extreme poverty currently plaguing areas in Eastern Asia. She suspected he'd only suggested the distraction to keep her mind occupied.

Visitors were few and far between at Marsh Manor. Any friends she'd thought to possess had long been married and now had their own families to care for and were, therefore, not concerned with the grave injustices around the world nor continuing a friendship with a woman who now verged on being a social outcast. At twenty years of age, Patience had danced her way through three Seasons before setting her sights on other activities to fill the endless days—far more noteworthy and pressing matters than what color was fashionable during the current Season or what lord every marriage-minded mum desired to set their caps on for their unattached daughters.

Not that she verbally admonished those who filled their every waking moment with such drivel—regularly, at least.

Her only reprieve from her causes was her rakehell brothers—and the mischief they found, even though they were both past the age of childish games. Her sisters, bless them, had both turned into tedious shells of their former selves, preferring to spend their time on the trivial matters of societal life, the exact things that Patience had, for lack of a better word, no *patience* for.

Patience took a few steps toward Merit's door before glancing across the hall to Valor's bedchambers. No light could be seen in the space between the bottom of the wood and the polished floor. Odd, her brothers never went anywhere without one another. They were joined at the hip, as her father liked to jest—thought Patience sometimes called the pair joined at the brain, as they seldom had any original thoughts between them.

But, as her sisters were always eager to remind her, it only mattered that a gentleman was pleasing to the eye—and heavy in the pockets.

Merit and Valor were most assuredly dashing young men with ample funds provided by Patience's father. She supposed a handsome exterior, large, deep pockets, and sense to use both wisely would be a rare combination indeed.

Patience grasped the latch to Merit's door and pushed it open, her smile still wide.

The alarming speed with which her grin faded, and the swift awareness of her scantily clad appearance gripping her would have caused all her siblings to fall upon one another in unrestrained merriment.

Her skin flushed warmer than a late August afternoon spent rowing on the clear, placid waters of the lake at her father's country seat—and, at the same time, a tremor caused her grasp to slip from the latch.

Perhaps she should have knocked.

Or, preferably, remained safely abed.

Before her stood a man, not one of her brothers that she still pictured as boys even though they were two and four years her senior, but instead a true man—stripped to the waist, his back to her.

Thank the heavens above for small miracles.

But to deny that her heart skipped a beat—or ten— would be preposterous. In fact, as Patience stood, unnoticed, studying the man now looking out Merit's open window, she wondered if her heart would ever beat a normal, steady rhythm again or if her skin would ever cool enough to need an overcoat or shawl. It was only when her lungs began to burn that she realized she'd held her breath since opening the door, a call of greeting stuck in her throat.

One utterly forgotten.

So intent on the window, the man failed to notice he was no longer alone.

There was no denying the stranger's presence—an unfamiliar masculine air filled the room. It was both intriguing and frightening. Certainly, she'd witnessed men in various stages of undress, but this goliath was different. Never had Patience been so utterly aware of her own body, while distracted by the sight of another's chiseled form. Her hands itched to reach out at the same time they should be raising to cover her exposed flesh, veiled only by her thin nightshift.

Patience was commonly overcome with indignation, rage, and resentment for those gentlemen who ignored the troubling aspects of society. Emotions she knew well, and how to hide and suppress them. Never had she been attracted to a man, or filled with such...euphoric pleasure at the mere sight of a bare back. Her nipples puckered...if that were even something possible for her womanly buds to do. Her knees trembled, though not with outrage and anger but...titillation.

Voyeurism.

It was what her father had explained drew the large crowds to prized pugilist matches all over the world—and to a certain extent, every *ton* gathering in the country.

Any other day, Patience would have adamantly and vehemently denied that she possessed any amount of voyeuristic impulses. Perhaps she could still claim this to be true if she stepped back over the threshold and silently closed the door, putting an end to the stark, raw nature of the sight before her.

The raw, stark emotion coursing *through* her.

The sensible thing would be to return to her room and never speak of this moment. Deny that it ever occurred.

That was the rational thing to do, and Patience always prided herself on her intellect, even though many in the *ton* considered a female with a mind something to be avoided at all costs.

The man raised his arms high above his head and stretched until he nearly touched the thick wooden beams overhead. He must be at least a foot taller than Patience and stand a head above both her brothers. Damnation, but the width of his shoulders seemed wider than she was tall. Heat pooled at the apex of her thighs as the muscles along his back tensed before relaxing when he put his hands on the windowsill and leaned slightly out to look down the two stories to the garden below.

She knew the view he took in well, though the cover of night with its cloud-covered January moon would mask the thicket of overgrown rosebushes below. It was the same scene she beheld when she gazed out her window in the bedchamber bordering this one. The roses were the only things daring to grow in such a wayward manner. The lawn was perfectly manicured and awaiting a garden party that would never take place. The small hedge maze, truly just five intersecting pathways at the back of their property, was only as high as it was to block the sight of the mews beyond. One side of the lawn, farthest from the stables, was lined with neatly pruned fruit trees that were dormant this time of year, while the other side had been converted to a long-unused sparring area for either fencing or boxing.

Shaking her head, she cast aside all her thoughts about voyeurism and the sights to be beheld outside her window.

There was a man—a stranger—half naked, in her brother's room.

"Sir"—Patience swallowed as the man turned to face her and the heat that had overtaken her face and neck—"please announce yourself and the reason for your presence in my home."

Patience immediately regretted calling the man's attention as his eyes narrowed on her and she took in his battered face: split lip caked with dried blood, knot on his forehead, and the bridge of his nose slightly rounded, betraying the swelling that would be present come morning.

Thankfully, none of the injuries had blemished his chest, or at least, Patience could not see any bruises through the light dusting of hair that covered his flesh. However, she did note the muscles that had rippled across his back and shoulders were also present on his front. In that moment, she'd almost convinced herself that she was scrutinizing nothing more than a prized horse or a champion hunting dog—not the alluring form of a fierce, red-blooded man.

He stared at her, his lips pressed into a grim frown. For the first time, Patience fretted that the man was in her home with dastardly devious and threatening intent. He did not appear a common thief, the likenesses of which were prominently displayed in the *Post* nearly every day. Nor was he outfitted as most burglars would be, with a shirt or tunic or something to cover his tanned chest and board shoulders, and likely something covering at least a portion of his face. He also did not take an aggressive stance or look about with frantic, piercing glances for a weapon or path of escape.

If anything, when his eyes latched on to her, his confidence filled her with an unbelievable sense of rightness.

Yet, it was not right for a stranger to be in her home at such a late hour clothed as he was, nor was it acceptable for Patience to be frozen before him wearing nothing but her nightgown.

Absolutely nothing about her current situation should feel fitting.

It was only when his eyes went from narrowed and assessing to wide-eyed before he turned and averted his stare that Patience regretted her less than suitable attire. Her night shift, while warm, was still white, and she had no corset or other modern device to hide the evidence of her perking nipples through the fine fabric. Could he see that she hadn't so much as donned a pair of the knickers that were becoming so popular in society?

Heavens, her face flamed with heat once more. This was *her* home, and she need give no explanation for her nightly attire.

"S—s—s—ir." Patience loathed the way her voice broke and stuttered over the single word. Taking a deep breath, she began once more. "I asked that you announce your name and purpose in my home."

While she spoke the words without stumbling, they did not hold the warning she'd hoped. They came out as a plea, not the demand she'd intended.

He refused to glance back in her direction, and Patience took the opportunity to take in her brother's room; everything was in its place except for the shirt tossed over a chair near the bed. Red stained the otherwise pristine white linen.

Were his injuries graver than first noted?

"Are you hurt?" She despised the empathy in her tone.

"I was preparing to leave." The deep lilt to his voice sent another wave of pleasure through her as his eyes finally met hers.

"You cannot leave in such a condition," she chastised. How many stories had her mother shared with her about the destitute in Seven Dials perishing due to the cold weather? "You will surely freeze before arriving at your intended destination—although, the frigid temperature will most likely slow the swelling in your nose."

Why in heavens was she giving advice, all but offering to tend the man's wounds, when he was an interloper in her home? He'd still not given his name or his reason for being in Merit's chambers in the middle of the night—not to mention his careless action of opening the window and allowing the coveted warmth to escape into the cold outside.

Oddly still, while he didn't appear scared that he'd been discovered, he *was* nervous and uneasy. She saw it in the way he took quick, shallow breaths and how he leaned forward, tightening his grip on the windowsill, turning his knuckles white.

Patience wasn't as frightened as she should be, though, again, common sense told her that she would be wise to flee the room and seek out the butler—or sound the alarm to wake her father. However, something held her in place and kept her mouth shut as she watched him. Pushing his hair back from his face, he leaned back in and turned to face her.

His hair, sun-kissed—that peculiar color between brown and blond—was long and hanging free like that of a man better suited for the high seas as opposed to civilized London society. On any other man, it would have appeared unkempt, and Patience would have recommended a cut; however, on *this* man, it would be a sin to do away with his long, shiny locks. Hair such as his certainly guaranteed envious looks from every female who passed.

The stranger moved with such swiftness that Patience hadn't a moment to speak before he snatched his soiled, blood-stained shirt and crawled out the window.

She'd been ever so taken by the broadness of his shoulders, the glossiness of his hair, and the expanse of muscle across his bare chest and back that she'd allowed him to escape.

Escape? That wasn't the correct word at all.

Patience hurried across the room and tilted forward out the window. He'd likely misjudged the distance to the ground and was now lying stuck, or worse, injured in the overgrown rosebushes. However, there was no one below. Placing her hands firmly on the window ledge, Patience stood on tiptoes and leaned farther out, looking from side to side down the wall of their townhouse. She spotted the man where he balanced himself on a small strip of wood above the parlor window below. As she stared, he leapt over the tangled, thorny bushes and landed in a crouch on the lawn before looking around and taking off in a sprint toward the drive that led to the front of Marsh Manor.

Not once did he glance over his shoulder—or up at her above.

There was no reason that should hurt her, but it did.

Who was the man, and what had he been doing in Merit's bedchamber in the middle of the night?

Just as quickly as she'd found him, he disappeared.

Footsteps echoed in the corridor, and Patience swung away from the window in time to see her father and their family physician, Dr. Durpentine, enter the room. The tall, thin man wore round glasses that were forever slipping down his nose as he worked. Patience knew the doctor better than most of the *ton* she was acquainted with as he'd been the sole physician who cared for her mother during her final years as the headaches increased and the memory loss and confusion set in.

"Lady Patience," the physician greeted, his sleep-tousled hair the only indication that he'd been deep in slumber before being summoned to Marsh Manor. "I did not expect to see you on this trip."

"Good da—evening, doctor." Patience crossed her arms over her chest, suddenly feeling exposed. "Father."

Her father turned sharply toward her. "Sweet pea? What in heavens are you doing awake at this time of night?"

Could it be that he hadn't noticed her when he entered the room behind the physician? She was well aware of his distracted nature over the last several years—truly, since they'd lost her mother—however, this was extreme, even for him. Perhaps Patience should speak with Dr. Durpentine about the situation.

"I heard a noise, and it startled me awake," Patience explained. "I thought mayhap Merit and Valor had returned home earlier than expected. Who was that man, Father?"

She tried to keep her words unbothered and light, as if the man didn't actually interest her beyond knowing who was responsible for disturbing her rest. Her father knew better than to believe her disinterest as his mouth pressed into a firm line and he silently debated whether or not to give her any information. She'd seen the look all her life. When her mother began to worsen, he'd anguished over how much to tell his children. Each time she asked him how it had gone distributing her pamphlets, he wrestled with how to answer. When she'd asked why no gentlemen ever asked her to dance during her final Season, he'd silently deliberated how to respond. Patience was always saddened to be the cause of his constant inner turmoil, yet she couldn't help but love him all the most for his fierce protectiveness.

Finally, he sighed. "On my way back from Delforte's Hell"—he never shied away from naming the establishments he visited with her pamphlets—"I happened upon a scuffle in an alley. The man...what happened to him, by the way?"

"He leapt out the window." Patience gestured toward the open bank of windows at her back. "Crawled down the side of the house and fled."

"Oh, interesting." The earl shook his head. "Well, I happened upon him and another man, a true n'er-do-well, in an alley. It appeared the thief had set upon him, and I stepped in to assist. Brought him here so Dr. Durpentine could see to his injuries."

The physician chuckled, pushing his glasses higher on the bridge of his nose. "It appears I am no longer needed."

Her father clapped the man on his back with a laugh. "Appears not. I'm confident he'll find a way back to the Albany. We can't help those who do not want our help, now can we?"

"We cannot, my lord."

"Please close the window and run along back to bed, sweet pea." Without waiting for her reply, he turned and ushered the doctor from the room. "May I offer you a drink for your troubles?"

Patience stared at her father's retreating back as he and the physician crossed the threshold and their footsteps retreated to the stairs.

Nothing about her father's detached attitude shocked or concerned her—it was his way of things. However, bringing a stranger—a man, no less—into their home in the middle of the night was very concerning.

Belatedly, she realized she'd forgotten to ask her father for the man's name.

ABOUT THE AUTHOR

USA TODAY Bestselling Author Lauren Smith is an Oklahoma attorney by day, who pens adventurous and edgy romance stories by the light of her smart phone flashlight app. She knew she was destined to be a romance writer when she attempted to re-write the entire *Titanic* movie just to save Jack from drowning. Connecting with readers by writing emotionally moving, realistic and sexy romances no matter what time period is her passion. She's won multiple awards in several romance subgenres including: New England Reader's Choice Awards, Greater Detroit BookSeller's Best Awards, and a Semi-Finalist award for the Mary Wollstonecraft Shelley Award.

To connect with Lauren, visit her at:
www.laurensmithbooks.com
lauren@Laurensmithbooks.com

Made in the USA
Monee, IL
23 June 2022